ROSE OF DANCÉ

A Novel

By Erika Sams

Chapter One

A Kingdom Like No Other

Close your eyes, open your mind and imagine the most beautiful world since Eden. Grass so green and spotted with flowers of every color, basking under a golden sun. Through the fields run children, their bare feet alive with dance, their laughter singing in the wind.

Now take flight with the birds, high above where the children play and see a vast, beautiful kingdom beyond the fields. Walls and homes of carved white stone, draped with climbing roses and ivy. The streets stir with joyous commotion. Upon a hill, perched by a cliff that drops to a roaring ocean sits the most glorious castle made of pearl and trimmed with gold. From the balcony of the castle, you can hear the waves of the sea collide with the cliff. The castle nearly glows in the light of the sun. This is the Kingdom of Dancé.

Just by imagining you can already see this kingdom is unlike any other. But its beautiful setting and the artistic details of the castle are not the only things that make Dancé a wonder. The entire kingdom is always alive with song and dance. Oh, the dance! Far and wide, from the young to the very old, it controls and consumes them, a great energy flowing from their souls to their feet. More than tradition, it is in the blood of every child born in the great Kingdom of Dancé. The kingdom of dance and song.

But no matter how graceful or swift, the commoners do not hold a candle to the royal family. When they take the ballroom, everyone halts in amazement at the power of each movement. Standing together or alone, the poise, the grace, the perfect ripple of the queen's dress as she twirls in the arms of her king—there is nothing in the world more captivating or beautiful.

In fact, it is said that those born of royal blood don't even need lessons. As they learn to walk as children, so they learn to dance, the steps coming as naturally as a baby's first breath—if you dare to believe such things.

The royal children are also born with a pink birthmark on the outer side of their right ankle. It is in the unmistakable shape of a rose—the Rose of Dancé—and never fades.

Never before and never again will there be a place more abounding in joy, hope, and peace. It is the envy of all others, though the Dancé natives never notice, too wrapped in their dream to let anything or anyone penetrate their happiness.

~

Through the laughter, a loud cry was heard from the castle, echoing off every wall in the kingdom. The queen gave one final push, and her child let out her first cry.

"She's here," the midwife said, wrapping the screaming princess in a blanket. "A girl."

"A daughter," King Michael breathed out in amazement from beside his wife. The midwife placed the little princess on her mother's panting chest.

"Christine," Queen Anna said in joyous relief between panting breaths and glistening tears. "My beautiful daughter."

Tears of joy were in the eyes of the king as he bent his face toward his girls. "I thought the Lord had already blessed me more than any man. He has outdone Himself."

Anna leaned back on her pillow to look up at her husband. He stroked her moist forehead with his thumb, drinking in the sight of her. His wife's slender arms so strong around their child settled peacefully in her mother's arms, recovering from the ordeal of birth. Anna's eyes the blue of crystal or the clearest ocean water. So tired and still so beautiful. Her hair so blonde it was almost white, damp from sweat, draped across her pillow in cascading waves. Her fair skin flushed pink from labor.

Michael's eyes were a deep sea-green and always seemed to sparkle with light. His thick, golden blond hair reached down to his broad shoulders. He was a full head taller than Anna, his body strong and fit beside her slender frame. His skin was tanned dark, his hands rough from wielding sword and shield.

The queen looked down at the baby whose thin pink lips opened in search of milk. Puffy eyes softly closed, and frail wrinkled hands settled on her mother's breast.

"She's perfect," Anna said.

"And beautiful like her mother," Michael smiled. "She looks just like you."

Anna blushed at her husband's words. "And she'll be strong like you," she proclaimed with certainty.

When Anna began nursing, the initial pain passed enough for her to breathe, the king lifted the blanket to see Christine's ankle. "She bears the mark of Dancé," he said proudly, running his thumb over the pink rose on Christine's soft skin. "The Rose of Dancé will live on forever."

The queen rested her head on her pillow and closed her eyes, a happy moan escaping her as the baby princess continued to suck milk from her mother's breast. The king gave his wife a soft kiss. "You did wonderfully, Anna. You are stronger than any man in my army. When you have rested, the entire kingdom will come together for a great ball to celebrate the birth of our new princess. These walls will fill with song and dance beyond anything in our history. People in every corner of the world will hear of this celebration and join in our rejoicing."

A smile pulled at the corner of Anna's mouth, and she gave an even quieter moan of gladness. Michael returned her smile and kissed her forehead softly. "Rest, my love."

As she drifted to sleep, the midwife took Christine to wash her in the far corner of the room with the help of two servants. Michael climbed in the bed beside his sleeping wife and waited anxiously to hold his daughter. Finally, she was placed in his arms, wrapped in a warm blanket. As he held his sleeping child, his queen curled peacefully beside him, Michael knew if there was ever a perfect moment in life, it was this one.

~

From every side of the castle, golden trumpets sang out a triumphant chorus. Rich purple silks hung from every trumpet, the players all in the same purple tunics adorned with the Royal Rose crest in gold on their chests. The flag of Dancé flew prouder than ever before. It was a perfect day. Warm sun shone over the land, the pearl-white castle glistening in its light. It was six weeks since the trumpets sang out the joyous news of the princess' birth, and now they beckoned everyone for a celebration. By the time the sun fell, everyone in the land would have come together for a ball in the great castle.

In the streets, everyone was in a glorious scurry of preparation. Ladies pulled out their finest tulle and silk gowns, some newly made for the occasion. Men carried messages and gathered food for the great feast. Grapes, berries, beans and every leafy green were piled high in baskets. Chicken, lamb and beef rested on gleaming wooden boards. Wines were brought up from the cellars and cheeses from the cheese house. The bakers ran through clouds of white flour as they beat dough into soft breads and fine cakes.

In the great ballroom, purple silk drapes hung from every pillar and swung from the balcony gate. Vines wrapped around the tall pillars adorned with roses. A small band set up their stringed instruments, tuning and practicing for the dancing, which would take place in mere hours. Countless cooks and kitchen helpers rushed around, setting long tables where food was piled high for guests.

Among the chaos moved David, the king's right-hand man and dearest friend. As children, David and Michael were like brothers; now David was Michael's most trusted advisor. In contrast to Michael's blondness, David had dark, nearly black hair in thick locks. He was about a foot shorter than his friend, fit but lean, and prided himself on the ability to disappear into nooks and crevices no one else knew about. Hide and seek was a pointless endeavor when they were children; eventually, Michael learned to let his friend hide, then run to his own pleasures. David would inevitably emerge around dinner time. No one ever knew from where. In fact, to this day there were places in the castle only David knew.

Times had changed. Instead of hide and seek, they had royal responsibilities. Whatever Michael needed, David accomplished as his aide. Today, it meant pulling off the most magnificent ball of all time. He was inspecting, instructing, chiding the slow and encouraging the anxious. His legs never stopped moving, racing through the ballroom to the kitchen, checking everything to make sure it was perfect.

"You're going to trip over your own feet before the night is through," Tony, the royal baker laughed as David swept past him for the eighth time in an hour, choking in a gust of flour.

David laughed but had no time to stop for remark, though he did pause long enough to dip his finger into a bowl of fresh icing, sneaking a taste on his lips. Moaning at the sensation of sugar and crème, he pushed open the kitchen door and was gone.

No one baked cakes like Tony. Everything was sure to be nothing short of divine!

As David raced down the hall with plans to meet with the royal massager, his wife cuts him off. "Please dear, take a breath and small drink of water."

David smiled into her green eyes and accepted the cup from her delicate hand. She watched him gulp the water like a man lost in a desert without drink for days. Her small mouth smiled and she giggled at him, long, dark curls bouncing around her shoulders. She was a short woman, though her strong build and confident stance left no question she could hold her own. Her skin is almond brown from the sun, and her square face glows with a joy that never faded.

David finished the drink, his eyes pressed together, embracing the cool liquid down his throat. He felt calm for the first time in days.

Finding the bottom of the cup, he handed it back to Elena and smiled gratefully. "Whatever would I do without you?"

"The entire kingdom relies on you. You've got to have someone to keep an eye on you too." She giggled her all-too-contagious giggle that never ceases to make David's heart soar.

Smiling broadly, he placed his hand on her cheek. "God, how I adore you, woman."

She grinned sheepishly and he kissed her lips firmly before dashing past her, leaving her swooning and breathless in the hallway. She leaned against the wall, her eyes following him as he disappears.

~

Anna stood on the balcony of the royal bedroom, looking out over the cliff at the roaring ocean and blue sky. It was beautiful and clear, the blue broken only by the bright yellow sun warm on her skin. Everything felt right. The wind blew through her hair and across her skin, picking up the tulle of her dress. She closed her eyes and breathed in deeply. The scents of flowers and salt tickled her nose and she smiled in perfect peace.

Hands glided around her waist, and she felt Michael's chin rest in the crook of her neck, his warm breath on her skin. Gazing out at the scene before them, they rested in the moment.

"I wish we could just stay like this forever," Anna said.

Michael nuzzled his face in her neck and kissed it. "I won't move until you pry me away."

Anna turned in his arms to wrap her slender arms around his neck and gaze into his eyes, their bodies pressed close together.

"I love you, Anna."

"I love you, Michael."

Michael bent and kissed Anna sweetly, the wind sweeping around them. The moment ended abruptly when a loud knock on the door drew their attention. Michael sighed. "We aren't finished."

Anna giggled, and Michael reluctantly let go. "Enter," he called.

David and three of Anna's handmaids moved in as fast as an ocean wave to the shore, "My lady, we must get you bathed and ready," David told Anna.

"I suppose it is time, isn't it?" Anna gave a glance back at her husband with a slight curve of her lip and followed her maids to the bath chamber.

David looked Michael up and down in assessment. He was wearing loose leather trousers that were covered in dirt, along with his boots. His white undertunic was untucked and wrinkled from sleep and his hands looked like he had been digging in the dirt. "Well, clearly you are ready for a party," David stated sarcastically.

"Come with me, my friend," Michael said gleefully and was out the door, a near skip in his step.

"But I don—" he began to object, but then thought better of it. Dropping his head with a useless sigh, he followed Michael down the steps, through the corridor and out the back to the garden.

The garden of Dancé was quite possibly Heaven on earth. From the moment you opened the door, you were in a wonderland. A stone pathway broke through green grass, and along the path, rose and other bushes and blossoming trees enraptured the viewer with the most beautiful flowers of every kind and color. A song like that of angels came through the leaves, sung by wind and birds.

The men walked along the path peacefully taking in the sight till they came to the end where once there were two white swings hung from a branch, entangled with vine and purple flowers. Now the two were joined by a third, smaller swing.

Understanding, David turned to Michael and asked rhetorically, "For Christine?"

Michael smiled proudly. Stepping carefully to the grass beside the swings, he knelt beside a recently turned patch of dirt. Out of the middle there sprouted a small tree, about a foot and a half tall. Michael tapped the dirt with his hand. "I planted it this morning when I also hung the swing. It will grow with Christine." He ran his fingers along a frail branch. "One day she will swing from its limbs, showing she is stronger than any tree—or any man. As its roots grow deep into the ground, she will be rooted deep in her Lord."

"It's beautiful," David said honestly. "She will treasure it."

Michael rose and looked around the garden. "This tree will live on, along with her memory, for generations."

Michael walked into a thick brush and pulled out a curved metal plaque. "I had this made. When the tree grows to its full size, it will be welded into the tree."

David looked at the plaque and read:

For Princess Christine of Dancé

Presented by your father, King Michael.

May your life be full of all the love and happiness

This world holds.

I love you

"It is a beautiful tribute," David said. "She will never be forgotten."

"No. Tales will be told until she is a legend."

~

The trumpets sounded as the sun trickled gold across the rippling sea. Under the setting sun, the people of Dancé were just coming alive with the evening's excitement, all ready to see their new princess.

Through the castle gates, fair ladies and gentlemen, giggling boys and girls all danced their way into the castle. Along the great halls and in the ballroom were lights, color, music, food and dancing in no short supply. Not one hour in, and the walls were nearly bursting with all the excitement, people laughing, silks and ribbons fluttering. David skirted the edge of the dance floor, expertly missing arms and legs flung in the air. He laughed to himself in gleeful delight and pride; he had done well.

Across the room he spotted his bride smiling at him brightly. She was a vision of beauty that captured him. She shot him a teasing wink, and he moved quickly to her, scooping his arms around her waist, pulling her close. "Oh my lady, you look more delicious than the baker's cakes!"

She laughed at him, her head thrown back and hands on his chest. He took the chance to steal a kiss from her neck.

"Are you not supposed to be on duty, sir?" she scolded him teasingly.

He growled and let her go, her sparkling eyes watching him.

The music grew fainter in David's ears as he stole away, making one last check on the king and queen before their entrance. The clicking of his shoes echoed down the hall. The sound of a woman's giggle surprised him; he saw a young couple run across the corridor to hide. He grinned and continued forward, the joy of the night warm and alive in his chest.

He reached the royal bedchamber and knocked.

"Enter," the king commanded.

David walked in to see the king standing over his daughter, pride in his eyes.

"Are you almost ready for your entrance, Your Majesty?"

The king's eyes did not leave his sleeping child, "So much bustle for such a tiny bundle. A perfect, beautiful tiny bundle. I want to proudly show her off to the whole kingdom, and by the same token, I want to let her sleep and just watch her peaceful breathes and pink cheeks."

David approached his friend, eyes moving to look where the king was entranced. The baby princess lay in a small bed of white that seemed large in comparison to her tiny body. A lace-trimmed gown draped loose around her body, her baby arms spread out in bliss. Her cheeks were pink from the warmth of her bed, fluffy blond hair barely visible on her smooth head and the tiniest button nose in the middle of her face. Her thin lips lay open in sleep with not a single care in the world. "She is beautiful," David agreed.

The door opened, and the queen entered. Both men jerked their heads from the baby to look at her. She was dressed in a long purple gown, tight in the bodice and loose in the skirt, draping down to her shins in the front while falling to the floor behind her. The flowing skirt allowed her to dance freely. Her blonde hair was half up in a loose bun to keep it off her face, the rest of her curls draped gracefully down her back. Her cheeks were dusted with powder, crystal-blue eyes popping from under long lashes and lined lids, her full lips pink with stain.

"You are a vision, my love," the king breathed, approaching to take her hand and kissing it gently. Her eyes batted up at him shyly.

"You do look very beautiful, my queen," David agreed from behind them.

"You gentlemen are too kind to me," Anna giggled.

Offering his arm, Michael asked, "Beautiful Queen Anna, will you do me the honor of dancing with me?"

Anna wrapped her arms possessively around his. "What about Christine?"

"She is sleeping so peacefully; let her rest while I dance with my queen and David will alert us when our princess is ready to meet her people."

Anna hesitated, thinking hard about the invitation and the idea of leaving her baby, even for a short time.

"Very well," she finally gave in. Then turning her attention to David, "But as soon as she wakes, send for me."

Her eyes flashed with a threat only a mother could give, and David bowed his head. "You have my word, Your Majesty."

Anna walked over and pressed a soft kiss to Christine's forehead. "I love you, Christine," she whispered softly. Then returning to her husband's arm, she let him lead her to the door.

"I'll send your wife to keep you company," Michael teased as they exited.

David smiled and assumed the position his king had claimed only minutes before, looking down on the tiny future queen, watching over her while she slept.

~

The sun had set, but the great ballroom was more alive than ever before. The king and queen approached the large doors for the royal entrance. Two guards dressed in uniform noticed their approach and reached white-gloved hands to the long handles. In a fluid motion, the tall golden doors opened, and the room went silent as a man called out, "Ladies and gentlemen, King Michael and Queen Anna of Dancé."

Michael and Anna stepped onto the upstairs balcony, the entire ballroom bowing low. The band began to play their entrance as they descended the stairs arm in arm. A line of people led to the dance floor. As the king and queen stepped out onto the floor, Michael lifted his wife's arm above her head and spun her around before wrapping his other hand around her waist. Looking deep into her eyes, he kissed her.

When he released her mouth, the music changed, and their bodies began to move as one. Everyone within the ballroom and looking down from the surrounding balcony was entranced. No matter how many times the king and queen took the floor, you could never be prepared for the grace, the power and the ability they showed. They provoked awe from beginning to end.

When the song ended, as the couple stood posed and breathless, the entire room erupted into shouts and whoops, hands clapping and joyful cheering.

When the crowd settled, the king and queen returned to their starting position, and the band began another song. One after another, couples linked together and joined their leaders on the floor.

Seeing the king and queen without their daughter, Elena smiled with a hint of humor and pride, knowing the only person they would have left her with. Sliding through the crowd, Elena made her way to the royal chambers.

When she opened the door, David looked up and welcomed her with a smile. "Hello, my beautiful bride," he said.

Coming behind him, she wrapped her arms around his waist and looked down at the still sleeping princess. "She's so beautiful, isn't she?"

Placing his hands over hers he said, "She is; she is perfect. Michael and Anna are so proud, as they should be. She will be a wonderful princess and a great ruler one day."

"So much responsibility to be born with," Elena thought aloud.

"If she is anything like her parents, she will be strong and able to handle whatever this life throws her way."

"What do you think our child will be like?" she asked.

David turned in her arms, wrapping his around her. "Our child?" he questioned.

Straining her head to look up at him, the edges of her lips tilted slightly. "Yeah, what do you think he or she will be like?"

His brow furrowed, and fingers tightened on her as he stared deep into her eyes, trying to determine if this was hypothetical, or if she was trying to tell him something.

"Elena?" he asked in an almost inaudible voice.

She gave a knowing nod. "I am."

He released a breath he hadn't realized was holding. Tears prickled his eyes, the biggest smile consuming his face. "We are going to have a child? Our child?"

Nodding even more, she said, "Yes, I was going to wait to tell you until after the party, but I couldn't wait anymore."

"Oh God, Elena," his voice was high. "I have no words."

"You're happy?"

"Happy?" he laughed. "I've never been happier in my entire life. We're going to have a baby. I'm going to be a father!"

Unable to contain himself anymore, he dipped his head and captured her mouth in a passionate kiss. His fingers tangled in her hair, her hands gripping the back of his coat. They lost themselves in each other. He pulled away long enough to say, "I love you so much," but didn't give her time to respond before taking her back again.

It was perfect. Everything was perfect. But they didn't know, in a single moment—everything was going to change.

Chapter Two

A Kingdom Falls

Across the sea lived the Demaras. They were unruly pirates who hated Dancé and everything good and happy it stood for. For many years they had plotted and built up their forces with men whose hearts were full of bitterness and hate. Their plan: to destroy the great kingdom and rid it of its wealth and glory. When word reached their captain that the king and queen had given birth to a child, an heir, he immediately gathered his forces and set sail for Dancé. The journey was long, but he had gathered a fleet of ships full of men armed and ready to bring the kingdom to its knees.

On the ship, the young men engaged in duels and elders planned. They hadn't spent so many years to fail in their mission. They sought one thing— complete destruction—and they were going to get it. Not a soul would survive.

It was night when the shore came into view. Every ship rowed in utter silence. The only sounds to be heard were boots hitting wood as they raced around, making sure everyone was armed for a swift takeover. As they got closer, they heard the music and saw the castle lit in celebration.

"They are having a ball for the new princess," the first mate told his captain. "Every citizen will be in the ballroom. It's almost too easy."

"Kill the royals last, but make sure they do not escape," he reminded. "If we kill them first, everyone will scatter. If we leave them till last, everyone will seek to save them, leaving them all trapped, right where we want them. No one escapes. No one survives."

When they reached the shore, it was dark. Gestures were made directing men to set cannons and take positions. Not a word was spoken until the entire kingdom was surrounded. They moved forward, checking every home as they crept with a silent deadliness through the kingdom. A few of the old and very young and sick had stayed home; they died first. Then they reached the castle where music rang out and lights lit every window.

An evil grin of sheer malice spread across the captain's face. "They're mine now."

~

David and Elena were embracing each other, looking down on Christine.

Downstairs, Michael and Anna laughed happily, clinking their crystal glasses together post-dance. Within the walls, every person in the kingdom, and some from beyond, mingled and danced blissfully. They were oblivious to the men flooding the halls, cutting throats and stabbing the backs of servants and guards. Finally, they reached the doors to the ballroom, throwing them open. There was no time to recognize what was happening until swords struck and blood spilled to the floor.

The music halted, replaced by panicked screams. Everyone tried to run, but they were surrounded. Dark-clothed, dirty, heavily armed men swarmed through every entrance, leaving no room for escape. Guards surrounded their king and queen, Anna clinging to Michael's shirt, his arms wrapped tightly around her, eyes searching for any chance to escape.

The people were unprepared, wrapped in their dance and freedom. It didn't take long for the pirates to murder their way through the crowd.

Upstairs, David and Elena were startled by the sound of screams. Elena began to shake violently, wide eyes looking up at David in fear. "What is happening?"

David crept quickly and discreetly to the window. Looking out from behind the curtain, he saw more than a hundred men around the castle gates and the sea spotted with ships shooting fire at the castle. "We're surrounded."

Immediately, he was on the move. "Get Christine!" He pulled Michael's sword from its stand and went to open the secret passage behind a large painting.

Elena had Christine in her arms, rocking her gently, praying to God she didn't wake. "What about Michael and Anna?"

"They will find a way out and meet us. We cannot delay, or it will be our death. They're counting on us to keep Christine safe. As of now, she is our only concern and responsibility. The guards will give their lives to bring the king and queen to us."

As he spoke, David grabbed two dark cloaks from the closet and an extra blanket before opening the secret door. Elena stood stunned, her legs like lead on the floor.

"Elena," he pulled her out of her trance. "We have no time. They will find us, but we have to get out of here first."

Inhaling deeply, Elena entered survival mode. Wrapping Christine warm and tight, she swiftly followed David into the secret passage. David grabbed a small lit candle and closed the door behind them, leaving the room silent and empty.

In the ballroom, surrounded, Michael and Anna had no options but to cling to each other. Their faithful guards were on every side, fighting for their lives. There was no way out, no escape.

"Christine," Anna said to Michael, in terror, her only concern their new baby.

"David will already have her out the passage. She will be safe," Michael assured her.

Tears filled Anna's eyes and she pressed into his chest. She knew he was right; already David and Elena would have their daughter in the underground tunnels heading for escape. This was the only thought that relieved her, and she said a silent prayer, thanking God they had not brought her down with them. Then a pain like nothing she had ever felt before stabbed through her heart. The last thing she knew was the scent of her husband's chest and his arms clinging to her with everything he had.

"No!" Michael screamed, falling to his knees, Anna's body limp in his arms. Around him, the guards fought with bravery and passion, killing and being killed—the beautiful ballroom turned from purple celebration to the red of blood and death.

Gasping for breath, Michael wailed over his wife, "No, no, Anna, don't go," but she was already gone. He gripped her body in his arms, burying his face in her hair, yelling from the pain. But it was only a moment of pain because a single stab in the back left Michael slumped dead over his queen.

The captain walked through the room, stepping over bodies, the last gasps and screams dying away as the men finished. His first mate came behind. "Sir?"

"Loot it then burn it," he ordered.

The men raged through the castle, taking the jewels, the silks, the gold and silver, the tapestries and small artworks. They didn't want to spend much time on it, but they got most of the treasure out, including several fine swords. Then oil was brought in and poured through the hall, over the bodies that lay dead and drowning the drapes. Moving backward to where they came in, the men left the castle stinking of blood and oil.

When everyone was believed to be out, a torch was brought and thrown at the oil. Flames rose instantly and followed the trail into the castle, through the walls and out the windows until the entire place was a single flame, reaching for the heavens. As the pirates left the city, they set fire to every home, leaving no one and nothing but destruction.

Dancé, the kingdom of joy, peace, beauty, and dance would be a pile of ashes by morning. With no care, the pirates continued their path back to their boats and returned to the ships, many staggering under chests of gold and jewels. As fast as they had swarmed the castle, they were gone.

~

David pushed the secret trap door above their heads and the cool air of night washed over them. Climbing the ladder up to the damp grass, he reached back to help Elena and the baby out. Following their exit, he covered the hole, and the rush of adrenaline left their bodies. Their faces went pale looking back at the kingdom—their home, their friends and family—going up in flame and smoke.

David fell to his knees, duty for the princess done, failure and heartbreak hitting him like lead. Elena just stood behind him, the sleeping child in her arms, mouth hanging open and tears streaming down both sides of her face. Neither could speak. Neither dare utter the truth they both knew—that Dancé was gone, and the only ones left were the three of them.

David dropped his face into his palms, clawed his hair, pulling, and then beat the ground with his fist. There was nothing he could do, nothing she could do, and the realization that they were now the guardians of the fragile queen who would depend on them entirely—never knowing her parents, maybe never even knowing where she came from—was unbearable.

How long they stayed there is uncertain, but the little cry of Christine waking to the cold pulled David and Elena out of their trance. Rising to his feet, David wrapped one of the cloaks around Elena's numb body, wrapped the other around himself and took the baby into his arms, wrapping the spare blanket to warm her.

"She needs milk," Elena finally spoke in a dead voice.

David nodded and put one arm around her waist, Christine temporarily settled in his other arm, baby blue eyes looking out at the dark night. David led them a few yards to where the emergency carriage was hidden. Knight, a black horse, tall and strong, let out a "Neigh" as David approached him. He released Elena long enough to rub the side of his neck. "Good boy," he cooed.

Offering his hand to Elena, he helped her into the carriage and then handed her the baby. "We will go as fast as we can to Hanton."

Elena nodded, still unable to speak, and snuggled Christine close to keep her warm.

David hopped into the driver's seat, snapped the reins, and they were off. They began fast, David unsure if the attackers would follow. When they were a good way down the road, he steadied.

Hanton was the neighboring kingdom, one that had a good relationship with Dancé. For generations, the doors between the two were always open, like brothers who stood by each other. They would be welcome, though the thought of explaining what had happened seemed impossible.

In the carriage, Christine began to cry. It was a quiet cry, soft and tender. It broke Elena's heart and she began to cry along with her. She wasn't her mother; she couldn't feed her. What would they do? Their home, the whole kingdom was rising in flames. Surely Michael and Anna had gotten out. They had to have.

Tears running down her face, wishing and praying, her heart shattered in a million pieces and terrified out of her mind, she was desperate to help the small child. Then, after what felt like forever, Elena's aching breasts wet her dress. Noticing, Elena's mouth widened, and her tears turned to relief. Her milk had come early from the baby's cries.

She could barely think, but at least she could feed the baby princess. Pulling down her dress, she snuggled the baby up to her leaking nipple. "Please, Christine. You can do it."

Christine's baby sobs went from uncontrollable to silent sniffs as her open mouth latched onto Elena in desperation. She sucked like she had never eaten before. Elena threw her hand to her mouth and bit down hard, trying not to scream from the pain, but she didn't push her away. She had never imagined nursing would hurt so much! Still, she was relieved she was able to feed the little princess.

"This will do until your mother finds us," Elena told the tiny baby whose content eyes were now staring up at her. "Because she's going to find us; I know she will. And everything will be okay." She wanted to promise but stopped herself. Could she promise? No. The last thing she saw of the kingdom was the fire sweeping over the castle and grounds. It would take more than a miracle for the royals to have survived. But she and David had survived, so maybe more people did too.

After Christine fed, the two of them snuggled up in the cloaks and blankets, the rock of the carriage steady, sending both of them to sleep.

~

The sun was creeping through the sky, spreading a low glow over the earth. David pulled into a hidden patch beside the road to let Knight rest. There was a creek he led the horse to for a drink. He found a couple of apples under the seat that he fed him. David rubbed and patted his neck. "Good boy," he spoke softly.

Tying the reins to a nearby branch so Knight could continue to drink, David walked a little way down the stream, close enough to see but far enough to be alone. The adrenaline was leaving his body, his legs going weak, his whole body beginning to shake. Giving in, he dropped to his knees in the damp grass, wet from morning dew. He clawed his fingers in the grass, finding the dirt with his nails, his teeth gnashing as an uncontrollable cry began to pour from him like the release of a dam. His chest heaved, bent down to the earth. He let out an angry sound that could only be described as a growl and then yelled, "Ah!" He looked up to the sky with his fists curled. He cried, he wailed, he sobbed until there were no tears and hardly any breath left in his body.

When he had regained himself, he moved to the edge of the river, dipped his hands in and splashed the cool, clean water on his face to clean it. Cupping his hand, he took a drink of the water and was still for a moment, finding his composure. He had a princess as well as a pregnant wife to protect, and as Christine was the only surviving royal from Dancé, that left David and Elena with the most important and dangerous job in the world.

Returning to the carriage, he found Elena nursing Christine, sleep still in Elena's eyes.

"Oh my God, you are able to feed her," he nearly breathed and cried out the words, shocked and relieved all at once.

"Yes," Elena near laughed. "I've heard of women dropping milk at the cry of a baby, even if they never had a child before, but I didn't believe it to be true until last night. She has been able to eat and so far is very comfortable. Though she will be better when her mother and father find us in Hanton."

David looked down at the ground. He wanted to think the same thing. He wanted to agree and say, *"Yes, they'll be right behind us. I'm surprised they haven't caught up yet."* But he knew it wasn't true. Even if his head wouldn't admit it, his gut coiled in grief.

For now, he chose to say nothing, just leaned in and kissed her forehead. "We are not far now."

Elena gave him a small smile, which he returned. Then he climbed back onto the carriage seat, taking the reins and urging Knight forward again.

Within a few minutes, David could see the plains of Hanton rising in front of him. Still over a mile away, it looked like a small house in the distance. Hanton was bigger than Dancé, though, its population easily double the small kingdom's, but they treated each other as equal and there stood no competition or haughty quarrel between them.

Hanton was a rich kingdom, its walls and castle lined with gold. An ally to all with pure intentions, Hanton was like the rich uncle to its neighbors. The king of Hanton was named Luke. He and his wife, Queen Tara, were both kind and generous, continuing the legacy laid down by generations before them. They had three sons, Thomas, Robert, and Daniel. The king and queen ruled with a gentle, though firm hand, and the people they served loved them.

This was where David and Elena would seek refuge. They did not fear being rejected, but the thought of having to explain why they were there—that the baby they carried was the princess; that the king and queen may not have made it through the attack—was unbearable. They both grew sick the closer they rode. The prosperous kingdom became overpowering. The walls were so high you had to strain your neck to see the top. David's hands shook as he approached, hating the awful responsibility that was upon him.

The large gates to the kingdom stood open, welcoming visitors. Tall men in expensive blue uniforms guarded the walls. When they approached, one of the guards walked up to the horse-drawn carriage as David halted.

"Good morning," David said.

"Good morning to you, sir," he replied. "Where are you traveling from?"

"We're from Dancé," David kept his voice steady and clear. "Our kingdom was attacked last night from the sea. We wish to speak to His Majesty and pray to find food and shelter as we wait for more survivors."

The guard bowed his head in sympathy. "I am sorry. Dancé has always been good to us. Please, make your way through to the castle. I will send one of my men ahead of you so they can expect your arrival."

The guard then saw Elena and the baby through the window. "You must need water. How long have you been riding?"

"We rode through the night," David told him as the guard made a commanding gesture to his men for some water, which was hurried over.

He handed the water to David and said, "Drink. There will be food and warm clothes when you arrive. May peace be with you."

"And with you, sir," David bowed his head. "Thank you."

David drank, gave the flask to Elena to finish and switched the horse to move on. One of the king's men had mounted his horse and was galloping through the busy streets for the castle. David was more at ease, grateful to have made it to Hanton safely.

Chapter Three

The Grace of Hanton

It took some time for them to navigate the busy streets. The hustle and bustle of a new day were in full swing, markets opening, maids shopping for fresh food and men selling their game. Barefoot children ran around in the front of their school, a game of tag filled with laughter. Elena's heart ached as she watched them, holding the orphan child in her arms. Just a day ago, that was what Dancé looked like. She dared not wonder if she would ever see life in their home again. If they'd ever be able to go back.

By the time they made it to the castle gates, their presence was expected. Guards ushered in their carriage, a stableman coming to collect it. David hopped down from the seat, opened the door and offered his hand to help Elena out. Her breathing was rapid and frightened, so he cupped her hand with both of his. "We have made it this far, my love," he said. "Breathe. We will get through whatever comes together."

He kissed her forehead, and she nodded before walking with him up the stairs.

The doors opened, and a plump maid with cheeks flushed as if she had been scurrying about all morning was there to greet them. "Sir, ma'am," she said with a small curtsy to both of them, "I'm Tilda;

you'll be in my care today. Oh, you both look so exhausted!" Pressing a hand to her stomach and one to her cheek, she assessed them both anxiously before hopping back into action. "Please, come with me." She was already moving as she spoke. "We will get you cleaned up, a good meal in you, and then when you're ready, His Majesty will see you. But not to rush, my dears; he does not expect you until this afternoon at the earliest. He wants you to be able to rest. Oh, to think of what you just went through!"

David and Elena followed behind her silently, Elena holding tightly to Christine, David's arm around her waist. They were both exhausted and could barely hear Tilda go on anxiously, leading them upstairs and down a long hallway as she did so.

"It's lucky you made it here so quickly and without a scratch on either of you." She did a quick check over her shoulder to confirm her words. "I just don't understand it. Oh, but listen to me go on and on." Reaching the room, she opened the door to reveal four more maids straightening the fresh sheets, opening curtains, laying out clothes, towels, and soaps. A sweet fragrance hit them immediately when they entered the room. It was enough to relax them just a little. They felt the warmth of gratitude in their weary bodies.

"I cannot thank you enough," David told Tilda, a heavy sigh of relief in his voice.

"None of that now," she told him. "Dancé is like a sister to us; we would do anything for those who grace us with a visit. I just regret it must be under these circumstances."

Elena looked at the ground, the weight coming back to her.

"Come in," Tilda pulled her out of it before she could fall too far. "We will get you bathed first. Our chef will be sending up some food shortly. Then you will rest."

The maid who was straightening the bed came up behind Tilda. She was an inch taller than Tilda and a little slimmer. She had long blond curls that were pulled behind her head and a kind face pale from spending most of her time indoors.

"This is Adela," Tilda told them, and Adela curtsied. "She will take your baby and bathe her so you can clean up."

Elena's grip visibly tightened on the princess, her eyes a little wide and fearful.

"Not to worry, darling," Tilda assured her, placing a gentle hand on her arm. "Adela has cared for plenty of youngsters. She will take the best care of your little one, and she will be returned to you as soon as you're all cleaned up and have had a chance to eat."

"You have my word, ma'am," Adela's small voice spoke up.

Elena looked down at the sleeping child. She was so peaceful, oblivious to how her life had just been flipped upside down. David placed his arm around her shoulder and spoke quietly into her ear. "It is okay, Elena. They will not hurt her, and you need a little time to care for yourself."

Elena nodded, tears of pain and relief starting to stream quietly down both her cheeks as she handed Christine to Adela.

"She will be back, bathed and dressed in fresh clothes when you are done," Adela assured her.

Elena nodded one more time, pointlessly wiping the floodgate that was now falling from her eyes and allowing David to pull her into him.

Tilda's words were then directed to David. "We've run a fresh bath; the water is plenty hot. Do you want assistance?"

"No, thank you," David shook his head. "I'll take care of it."

Giving a gentle smile, Tilda bowed her head and went for the door, gesturing for the others to follow her. When she clicked the door closed, David and Elena were left alone. Elena turned in David's arms, wrapping hers around his waist, burying her face in his chest and sobbing. David placed one hand on her back and smoothed her hair with the other, tears taking him as well. They had completed their duty. They had gotten the princess to safety and now faced the reality that their home, everyone they knew, and their best friends were all gone.

They stood there a while, until Elena composed herself, her face splotchy from her cry. Without words, David led her to the large tub, big enough for two. She let herself go limp as he began to undo her corset and remove the layers that covered her. When she was naked, he helped her gently into the tub and left her sitting there as he removed his clothes, put them aside and slid in behind her.

David took a small bowl that was beside the tub, dipped it in the warm water and began to pour it over Elena. She closed her eyes and let him wash her. When her hair was clean, she leaned back against him and just rested there, near sleep. He did not fight her; he had no desire to move either.

Before they fell asleep, though, he got them both out of the bath, dried her and himself and led Elena to the bed. Covering her in white linens that were soft to the touch, David climbed in beside her, their bodies sinking into the mattress. David pulled the thick blanket over both of them before spooning Elena. Nuzzling to her ear, he whispered, "Rest, my love. Let the worries wait until after you sleep."

He kissed the side of her head. She pulled his arms tighter around her in response, and within moments, they were both asleep. What they would face when they woke was temporarily forgotten.

~

Knock, Knock. David woke with a start to the gentle knocks on the door. He sat up and saw Tilda enter, a server with a tray of food behind her. "Hello, sir, you've been sleeping for a long time." She walked to the large velvet drapes, grasping their thick fabric and pulling them open wide, inviting in the sun.

David turned to look out the window. The sun was golden; it was probably late afternoon. Turning his attention to Elena, he saw she was still sound asleep next to him, her long dark curls cascading across her pillow and around her shoulders.

"Don't wake her just yet," Tilda told him gently, raising a hand as if to stop him. "We will just leave the food here."

The server left the tray on a small table near the bed. An overwhelming aroma of turkey and fresh bread filled the room. Two steaming cups of tea sat on either side of the metal domes that kept their food warm. David heard his stomach growl and realized he had not eaten in a day.

"Get dressed, eat some food, we will bring your baby back in here shortly," Tilda instructed, opening up the tall closet and pulling out black pants, a blue shirt and a modest but beautiful pink dress with white lace trim. She laid all of these out at the end of the bed. David was rubbing his face, trying to remove the sleep from his eyes. Turning to Elena, he began to rub her arm gently, causing her to stir and groan.

"My ladies have taken quite a liking to your tiny bundle. What is her name?" Tilda asked.

"Christine," David told her flatly, a sick feeling in his gut. *She's not mine,* he thought, but wasn't ready to say it out loud. The thousand questions of the next hours, days, years kept him from revealing anything until he had spoken with the king.

Tilda grinned. "Isn't that the name—" she trailed off, her face falling in horror as recognition of the situation consumed her. The realization that she had spent the day with the baby princess and that no survivors had arrived meant only one thing. Pulling her mouth back into place, she gave a kind smile and finished, "Well, Adela is taking good care of her, I promise you, sir," a new sincerity now in her sure tone. "Once you have eaten, we will bring her, and you can speak with His Majesty. He is anxious to see you both."

She gave a quick bow. David nodded. Then, clearly uncomfortable and embarrassed now, she disappeared out the door, leaving them alone again.

David sighed, pulling his knees up to rest his elbows and rubbed hands down his face. The situation was uncomfortable for him too, as well as heartbreaking. What were they going to do? There didn't seem to be anything left of the kingdom, the whole thing gone up in angry flames. And the king and queen? Still no word of any other survivors. He was sure they would have heard by now. Avoiding it wasn't going to change anything, though, so he threw the covers, standing out of bed and began to dress.

Elena rolled in the bed to look at him, her eyes half closed still and her voice groggy. "David?"

He moved beside the bed and kissed her head tenderly. "Time to dress, my love. They've brought food, and we will meet the king soon."

David grabbed the pants Tilda had laid for him off the bed and stepped into them, fastening them at the front before grabbing the shirt, the fabric soft and comforting against his skin.

Elena looked around, blinking the sleep from her eyes and assessing her surroundings. Her mind fogged; she tried to recall how she had gotten here. The memory of flames consumed her eyes and she jerked. "Christine?"

"They'll bring her to us once we have eaten," David told her as he finished tucking in his shirt. "Tilda assured me they are taking the best care of her. Apparently, all of the ladies have already grown attached to her."

Elena smiled, thankful for that one small solace. "Yesterday morning we were in Dancé, preparing for the most magnificent ball in our history. Yesterday everything was perfect. How can we be here now? In only a day, how has everything fallen apart?" She choked out the last words, tears brimming her eyes.

David sat beside her on the bed with a deep sigh, his eyes staring blankly at the wall. "I don't know, Elena. I—" he trailed off.

"David," Elena said his name softly and then paused. "What if—what if no one—"

David rose. "Don't go there," he cut her off. "Not just yet."

Elena rose silently and began to dress. Her heart wrenched, her gut beat at her. David tied the ribbons of her dress and then removed the metal dome from the food. The smell was so overwhelming, Elena immediately jerked her hand to her mouth and ran to throw up.

David ran to her, concerned. "Elena," he said, "are you alright?"

Sitting on the floor against the wall she said, "Tragedy and pregnancy do not mix."

David rested his hand on her stomach, thankful his unborn child did not know the pain they were experiencing. "Is there anything I can do?" he asked.

She shook her head. "No. But there is no way I can eat that."

David lifted her, guiding her to a nearby chair. Then he covered the food, grabbing a small piece of the warm, soft bread and a cup of water. He offered these to Elena. "Here. You must eat at least a little for our child's sake."

She nodded, taking a sip of water first and then nibbling sadly at the bread. Her stomach felt sick, but she forced it down. David grabbed some bread as well, along with the cup of tea and sat beside Elena.

"What will we tell the king?" Elena asked. "How will we say-"

"We will tell him the truth," David told her, "and trust his wisdom in how we move forward."

They both went silent, slowly eating as much as they could stomach, drowning in fear of what was to come.

~

In the evening Tilda returned to their room with an officer at her side and holding Christine in her arms. The care with which she walked and held the baby showed a whole new reverence for the child. She handed Christine to Elena, making sure she remained wrapped in the purple blanket she had swaddled her in. It was the same purple as her kingdom's flag, which David and Elena both noticed.

"Thank you," David told her sincerely.

Tilda nodded knowingly. "His Majesty is waiting for you in his sitting room. Stephen will take you there." She gestured to the unmoving man in full uniform, gloved hand resting on the hilt of his sword, dark eyes piercing both of them. He was almost frightening.

David put his arm around Elena's waist. "Come, it will be alright," he said, guiding her forward.

Stephen was the kind of silent that rang loudly in your ears. The stomp of his hard boots echoed off every wall. Anyone they passed would stop and bow their head to him. Finally, they made it to two large doors, guards standing before them.

"Sir David and Lady Elena of Dancé to see his Majesty," Stephen announced to the armed guards once he stood before them. His voice was deep and commanding like thunder.

The men at the door nodded and opened them.

The room was large, twice the size of the sitting rooms in Dancé. Pillars stood tall near the entrance. A large fireplace on the left wall, three sofas and eight high back chairs adorned the room, allowing many to sit and converse.

The king sat in the center chair, his queen in her seat beside him, relaxed over the arm. Two other men sat on either side. The one to the right of the queen was young and handsome. The one to the left of the king was older, the glaze of a long life in his eyes.

"Sir David and Lady Elena of Dancé, Your Majesty," Stephen announced, bowing from the waist to King Luke.

"Thank you, Captain," the king replied. "David, Elena, please come and sit. Captain, would like you to join us as well?"

"Thank you, Majesty." Stephen bowed again before taking a seat beside the older man.

David and Elena sat together on one of the sofas directly facing the king and queen.

"It is good to see you again, David," the king began. "I regret it is under these circumstances."

"Horrific as the circumstances are, it is always good to see Your Majesty," David replied.

King Luke was still young and healthy, not yet in his fifties. His face gave no sign of age. Only by the silver threading his dark hair beneath his crown might you suspect. He had a square face, thick neck and a tall, strong body.

"You remember my wife, Queen Tara," Luke gestured to his queen who lounged beside him.

"It is so good to see you again," she said, her voice royal and soft. She was a slender woman, tall like her husband, though he made her look small. Her fingers were long and adorned with many rings, and her neck too was draped in jewels. Her face was long, eyes like perfect almonds, slanted just so. Her lips pink and cheeks flushed. A crown that sparkled with many diamonds adorned her head. Her dark hair was up, nearly hiding the hint of silver. She was the picture of royalty.

"My eldest son, Prince Thomas," Luke said of the young man beside the queen.

Thomas bowed his head just slightly. He looked like a younger version of the king. Silver hairs were still years from touching his head, but he had the same square jaw and dark eyes. His body was strong, though not as broad as the king's. There was no doubt he was a prince.

"To my left is Major Reed and you've met Captain Stephen," Luke finished the introductions.

"It is an honor to meet you, sir," Major Reed nodded to David. "I've heard great things of what you do for His Majesty King Michael."

"Thank you," David acknowledged.

"Now," Luke said, his voice filling the room with authority, "tell us what has brought you here. I've heard a little, but I desire to hear everything directly from your witness."

"Yes, Majesty," David said, then glanced at Elena, who was looking at him with frightened eyes. He gave her a small smile and a squeeze of her hand before sitting perfectly straight on the edge of his seat and continuing, "Last night was the ball to welcome Princess Christine, the baby of the king and queen and heir to the throne of Dancé. Everything was perfect, our walls bursting with every citizen and friend. The king and queen did not want to wake the princess and went to dance and celebrate before bringing out the child. Lady Elena and I were watching over her in the royal chambers when we heard the sound of brutal screams, unlike anything I'd ever heard. I looked out the window to see we had been surrounded. Knowing our first duty was the protect the heir, we took the princess and escaped through the underground tunnel, expecting the king and queen to do the same. We were sure they would meet us—" he choked and stopped for a moment, swallowing hard to regain his composure.

King Luke waited patiently for David to continue.

"When we reached the end of the tunnel, we could see the entire kingdom," he paused. "It was completely consumed in flames. I do not know who else made it out. We have not seen anyone."

A silence filled the room as everyone took in the words David had spoken.

"This child," the major said. "She is the princess?"

David nodded, "Yes, sir."

Elena had quit breathing in anticipation of what was to come.

"You did what was right," the king finally told them. "Saving Princess Christine was indeed your duty at that moment and what her parents would have desired."

"I was sure if we got her out, it was only a matter of time before we were joined by others," David told him.

"You are the only ones who have reached Hanton so far," Major Reed told them. "We have sent riders to see what is left and if any other survivors can be found."

"Perhaps they simply have not made it here yet," the queen's sweet voice of optimism spoke.

"When are the riders to return?" King Luke asked.

"They were my fastest riders. I expected them back by sundown," Stephen said.

As if on cue, the doors opened and one of the guards entered. "Your riders have returned, Your Majesty." He bowed before moving out of the way.

Three men in dark, dusty clothing walked quickly inside. The one in the front, Smith, spoke. "Your Majesty." They all three bowed from the waist.

"Speak," said the king. "What were your findings?"

Smith glanced nervously at David and Elena before speaking. "Dancé has been completely leveled by fire. The flames are dying but not yet gone. We searched all around, calling out for anyone that could hear. We found no one. We were able to get into the castle. It was crowded with hundreds of burned bodies and ash. We did find one thing."

Smith turned to one of the men behind him and nodded for him to come forward. He walked to a small table by the fire, lifted a leather bag, removing items from it and placing them on the table. Elena gasped and covered her mouth, David squeezed her hand so tight she thought it might break. Two crowns burned black by fire and layered in ash.

Chapter Four

A Refuge Queen

"Cynthia." The queen gestured to her lady who stood in the back corner.

Cynthia scurried over and held out her arms to take Christine. Elena let her go without question, completely falling apart. The queen walked over and took Elena's hand. "Come, dear," she said softly, "let me take you somewhere quiet."

Elena nodded, unable to speak, and let Tara lead her out of the room.

When they had gone, Luke looked at David. "Do you need a moment?"

David's chin was set hard, his eyes staring at nothing, trying to pull himself together. He refused to fall apart; he couldn't. His duty came first. So he closed his eyes, inhaled deeply and said, "No, Majesty. I cannot sit and wait. The time to mourn will come. First, tell me what I must do."

Luke looked hard at David as if trying to determine if he really was able to move forward. Deciding, he nodded and turned his attention back to the riders. "You are certain there was no one else?"

"Majesty, I am yet to put my name on it, but as of now we have no reason to believe anyone else made it out."

"And there is nothing left, no home or castle?" the major asked.

"No, sir," Smith confirmed. "At its current state, it would have to be rebuilt from the ground up. It will be years before it is ever habitable."

"Thank you, gentlemen," the captain said. "Go wash from your ride."

The three of them bowed and exited.

The major spoke again. "Dancé is gone. With no survivors, I do not believe there is anything else to be done except pray for the souls lost."

David was immediately enraged; it took everything to contain his anger. "We survived. And so did the heir to King Michael and Queen Anna."

"It is true," Luke agreed. "The little baby would now be the queen."

"*Is* the queen," David put in. "As long as there is an heir, I will not give up on Dancé. His Majesty would want his daughter to receive her birthright."

"I understand your feeling," Major Reed replied, "but heir or queen, she has no kingdom to rule."

David ran his fingers through his hair in frustration. He didn't know what he had expected, and he heard the truth in Major Reed's words. He had hoped by the time he got here, there would be word of other survivors, word that the king and queen still lived and were ready to take their daughter home. This would not be the case, though, and he did not know what to do next or how he would do it.

King Luke was rubbing his chin thoughtfully. "Dancé has always been an ally to Hanton. We have had their back and they have had ours. Countless times have we found ourselves fighting side by side with our sister Dancé. I stood by King Michael in battle myself. He saved my life once, took a dagger in the arm to save me. I know if the roles were reversed he would do everything in his power to restore hope and peace to Hanton. Why would we not do the same?"

"Your Majesty, to rebuild an entire kingdom," Major Reed spoke, "would cost us dearly. Our forces would be weakened for a place and a people that are no more."

"We have the money," Luke said. "We have the resources and plenty of men to spare. What good is gold locked away? And men if they never work? Yes, it may take years before anyone can ever live there again. But it is fine rich land, not a desert to be abandoned. I know there are people here who would like land to farm; we have been straining our borders lately. And the baby queen is young. She can have a normal childhood here and when she is of age, perhaps we could give her the throne that was stolen from her in her infancy."

"But, sir," Major Reed objected again, "who would you appoint to oversee such a thing? Such a thing to ask anyone to commit to—"

"I will do it," Prince Thomas cut in. "I will oversee the reconstruction of Queen Christine's home."

Major Reed was stunned to silence. Luke's mouth pulled at the edges with pride. "So you shall, my son," he said.

"What until then?" David asked anxiously. "My wife and I, baby Christine. Until we can give her the throne, what shall be done with her?"

"It seems only right that Sir David and his wife raise the child," Stephen said.

"I agree," said Luke. "When Queen Christine comes of age, we will tell her everything. And we shall pray that by such time, we can return her home. Until then, she will simply be Christine, daughter of Sir David and Lady Elena. You will raise her as your own, so she may have a happy childhood. There is no reason to burden someone so young with this heartbreak."

David could not speak. He had avoided the thought of many of the things that might happen, but the thought of raising his queen as his own daughter—that he could not even comprehend.

"Your Majesty," the captain said, "are you sure keeping the truth from her is wise?"

"I am not certain of anything right now," the king told him. "Only weeks ago we received joyous news of this child's birth. We were all full of happiness. It is one thing to have a loss in war, but for these cowards to come in the night, no warning or chance for a fight—

" he paused. "I am certain of nothing, except that she is not old enough to know her name and yet she has lost everything. We will wait until she is of age, or if it is deemed necessary, before then."

No one spoke to argue with King Luke, which settled that. Then David said, "Your Majesty, what shall I do? Where will we stay? I—my wife, she is with child; I only found out yesterday."

"You will stay here in my castle," Luke spoke certainly. "And as for work, you will be on my council. Michael trusted you with his—with everything. And you proved yourself beyond any man when you saved his daughter from certain death. I believe you could be an asset, and when the time comes for Dancé to rise, you may return with no question."

"I am in your debt, Your Majesty," David said.

"I was in greater debt to King Michael," Luke said. "I would do anything for his child and dearest friend. Perhaps one day I shall even give my youngest to his daughter in marriage. Our offspring can rule together."

"Do not joke, Majesty," Reed said.

"Joke?" Luke scoffed. "I am as serious as the stars above. When that child grows, if she wants to marry a son of mine, I will die a happy man. They could rule together in the kingdom."

The door opened, and Queen Tara walked back in.

"How is Elena?" David asked, rising from his seat.

"She will be alright," Tara told him. "It will take some time, though. Tilda has taken her to rest."

"It has been decided that Sir David and Lady Elena are going to raise the baby queen until she is of age," Luke told his wife. "Until then, no one will know who she is except those in this room."

Every man nodded in understanding.

"We must do something to honor our friends who have been taken from us," Queen Tara said. "Tonight, let us release lanterns in their memory."

"Yes," Luke agreed. "Captain, send word for all arrangements to be made. When the sun has hidden behind the earth, we will release lanterns for our brothers lost in Dancé. Have your men send word throughout the kingdom."

Captain Stephen was on his feet, bowing. "Yes, Your Majesty. Consider it done."

Turning on his heels, he was out the door.

"David," Tara said, "my ladies have Christine; she is in very good hands. Go, be with your wife, take the time to mourn. We will send for you when everything is set."

David bowed to her. "Thank you, Majesty," he said.

He bowed to King Luke and then followed a waiting soldier out the door.

King Luke then turned to Reed. "Assemble your most trusted spies, I want to know who did this to Michael and Anna. There will by justice by my hand."

"It is done, Your Majesty."

~

Later that night, David and Elena were standing out on one of the castle's large balconies. The sun had set, leaving the sky black and speckled with tiny stars. Hands on the rail, Elena looked down below at the large crowd that had gathered, candles and torches making a glow all around them. Within the hands of everyone gathered were white lanterns, lit within, to release.

Luke came and stood behind them. David and Elena turned to face him.

"The night is too beautiful for this heartbreak," Luke said.

"Michael would have had it no other way," David told him.

Luke smiled, "You are right. And he would want you both to be happy. Do not give up on life in the wake of this tragedy. The men who did this win if your spirits break. Don't let that happen."

Tara came around the corner to join them, followed by two men holding four lanterns. In her arms she held Christine. "She deserves to see the lights that honor her family and kingdom," Tara said.

Luke nodded. "How right you are." He put an arm around her waist, taking the offered lantern in the other hand.

"They will never be forgotten," Elena said. "May their legacy be remembered, and the magic of the rose rekindled."

"We release these," King Luke said, "in memory and honor of King Michael, Queen Anna and every beautiful soul we lost in that heinous attack. We will never forget."

Luke released his lantern, soon followed by Tara, David and Elena. The lanterns glided high above their heads and went to find their own refuge in the sky. Within seconds, lanterns began to rise from down below, through the city streets and beyond. As far as the eye could see, small glowing lights were released and flew to make their home in the sky.

They stood there and watched in quiet reverence, holding each other close. Christine watched the light in awe, her eyes dancing, a small hand rising, trying to reach them. Not a word, even a whisper was spoken until the lanterns had joined the stars, becoming one with the sky.

For David and Elena, the future was more uncertain than ever. They would now serve in a kingdom not their own while raising the tiny queen to whom their loyalty was promised. Everything felt twisted, broken and wrong. How do you raise a queen without a throne? Without father or mother, without the place where she belongs? How do you explain where she came from and her purpose in this world? All they could do was live one day at a time. Maybe even one moment. Until one day maybe, things would be right again.

Chapter Five

Just A Girl

Ten Years Later

The sky was a perfect baby blue, the sun warm and bright, its rays shining down on Christine. She ran free and happy through the grass, her bare feet sinking into rich soil, long blonde curls bouncing behind her. She laughed and turned back to see her brother Jack, a year younger but almost as tall, his hair shaggy and dark, thin legs try to keep up with her sprint.

"Hurry up, slow poke!" she laughed at her brother, not stopping to let him catch up.

"One day, I'll catch you," he told her, giving it everything he had to go faster.

"Never!"

She threw her arms out beside her, turning in a graceful spin without losing momentum.

"How do you do that?" Jack called to her.

"I don't know," she replied. "My feet just take me."

She reached the tree they were racing for and immediately began to climb.

"I've got you now," Jack said. "You know I'm the better climber."

It was true. He didn't have her speed, but he could hide from wolves in a tree. Gasping for breath, they hopped on the tallest branch that supported them, Jack making it just as Christine did. They both laughed in childish glee.

They were facing away from the city, perched high in the tree where they could see for miles. "I wonder what else is out there."

"Trees," Jack said, "and somewhere beyond that, people. Father says no place in the world is as beautiful and happy as here though."

"Father says a lot of things," Christine scoffed. "You don't think about seeing for yourself? You don't imagine one day, when we are older, going to find out what is beyond those trees? Just taking your horse and riding until you have nothing left? Perhaps meeting a witch or a unicorn."

"Bedtime stories, Christine," Jack said, trying to sound older than he was. "When are you going to grow up?"

Christine gazed out at the world, her eyes sparkling with the possibilities. "The stories came from somewhere. Perhaps I would meet a prince, and he would fall in love with me. I would be his princess and we would live happily ever after."

"A princess?" Jack looked disgusted. "You could never be lady enough for that."

"I could!" she objected. "I would be the greatest princess there ever was."

"Prince Daniel seems to fancy you," Jack said.

"Prince Daniel will never be king," Christine said. "I would have to marry Prince Thomas."

"Prince Thomas?" Jack looked at her like her head had flipped around. "He's nearly thirty! And you're barely ten. Father would never approve."

Christine leaned on a branch looking dreamily at the sky. "I wonder where he goes on those long trips of his? He is gone for weeks, months at a time. Perhaps he goes to meet princesses, looking for a wife, and they're never good enough. Or fights filthy pirates at sea." She leaned her cheek to her hand with a swoon. "He is so dashing."

"Yeah," Jack laughed, "for an old man."

Christine scrunched her nose at him. "Have you no lady you fancy?" she asked.

Jack's cheeks went red, and Christine's eyes widened with a new excitement. "Oh you do, don't you? Who is she?"

"I'm not telling," Jack objected.

Christine squealed and clapped her hands. "I will have to look out for her now. Oh, it's so exciting."

"It's nobody," Jack tried to convince her, but she wouldn't hear it. She was lost in her happy dreamland.

A trumpet sound captured their attention. Christine clapped again. "Oh! Prince Thomas is back from his trip."

She was scurrying down the tree immediately.

"I wonder if he brought home a lady," Jack said, his feet hitting the ground seconds before Christine.

"Don't tease," Christine scolded, and they were both off.

She made it back to the castle gates just in time to see Prince Thomas pull his horse to a stop. "Whoa, boy," he told his horse and hopped to the ground.

"Well, hello, my lady," Prince Thomas said seeing Christine, her cheeks flushed from running and hair a frizzy mess. He bowed to her, and she gave him a curtsy back.

"Hello, Your Majesty," she greeted. "Welcome back."

"Thank you," he replied, taking a knee in front of her so they were level. "How is your family? Are you keeping that brother of yours in line?"

She giggled, "Yes, sir. If he does anything I don't like, I just run. He can never catch me."

Thomas smiled, "Good. Never hide your strength, not from anyone."

She nodded, "Yes, Prince Thomas."

Just then, Jack ran up behind Christine. "Hey, Prince Thomas," he greeted.

"Jack," Thomas bowed his head to greet him; Jack did the same. "Will the two of you be at the ball tonight?"

"Mother doesn't want me to go," Christine scrunched her nose. "But I'm ten years old now, nearly a lady." She straightened her back, lifting her chin high in an effort to look older.

Thomas laughed kindly at her. "Well, if you do come, promise me you will honor me with a dance."

Christine blushed. "Yes, Your Majesty."

"Good." He touched Jack's shoulder. "You look out for your sister."

"I always do, Majesty," Jack said.

Thomas rose to his feet, nodding his approval and mounted his horse to ride up to the castle. "I will see you both soon." And he was off.

Ever since the day David and Elena came with Christine to find refuge in Hanton, Thomas had felt very protective over her. She didn't know why he was so attentive. The truth was, he spent most of his days rebuilding her kingdom, and with every bit of progress they made, he grew more anxious to put that spunky little girl on her throne. It had become a very personal mission to him, and he put everything he had into its completion.

Christine and Jack watched him ride off, and she said, "Yes, I will most certainly be a princess one day. I was made for it."

~

That night was the spring ball in the castle. Everyone in the castle and many throughout the kingdom gathered to celebrate the first blooms. There was music, feasting, and dancing. Elena was not over what had happened ten years before and had refused to let Christine or Jack attend any previous balls. But that didn't keep Christine from continuing to beg, and that night as David, Elena, Christine and Jack all sat down to dinner, Christine would not let it go.

"Please, Mother," she pleaded, "just once let me go to the ball. I'm ten years old, nearly a grown woman. Just let me see it."

"You have plenty more years before you are full grown, my dear," David laughed into his wine glass.

Christine sighed. "Father, please talk to her. What will it hurt me going to just one ball? Long enough to have one single dance."

"Christine," Elena scolded, remembering it only took one ball to destroy the Kingdom of Dancé. "It is like you are not hearing me."

"She's not listening," Jack mumbled quietly into his food.

"I said no," Elena finished, "and that is final."

"But, Mother—"

"No."

"But even Prince Thomas invited me," she whined.

"Thomas? What do you mean?" Elena asked.

"Prince Thomas came home from one of his trips today, and he said if you allowed me to come, he wanted a dance," Christine explained.

"Did he now?" David asked, suddenly very interested in his wife and daughter's quarrel.

"He did," Jack responded. "Heard it with my own ears."

"Oh, what was he thinking?" Elena put her hand to her heart. The thought of Christine dancing, in front of people, was just as bad as the idea of her at a ball. It was all too familiar, in a nightmarish way. She feared, too, that those who hated Dancé were still out there and Christine could be discovered if she had even one dance.

"Mother," Christine said more calmly this time, "please, I promise I will leave when it's time for bed. Just let me go, just this once."

Elena paused to think, actually considering it this time. She knew what it was like to be young, to want to see a ballroom, lit by a thousand candles, full of music and pretty dresses, to want to dance. She had no wish to pass her own heartbreak to the child.

"Elena," David said from the end of the table, "it might be good for all of us if we let her go for a little while."

Elena understood what he meant, though she did not like it.

"Very well," she conceded, "until it is time for bed. But if anything should happen, or you try staying longer, you will not see another ball until you're thirty. Do we understand each other?"

"Yes, ma'am," Christine grinned, jumping up and giving her mother a hug. "Thank you!"

Not even bothering with the last of her supper, Christine ran out to go get ready.

"May I be excused?" Jack asked.

"Yes," David said. "Go ahead, son."

When he was gone, Elena slumped in her chair, picking at her food with her fork, but not eating any of it.

"I understand your fear, my love," he said to her gently. "I don't like it either. But she is safe here, and if we keep her away too much, she will catch on. She was given to us so she could have a normal childhood."

Elena looked at him from under the lids of her eyes. "It's just—"

"I know," David said, standing and moving to the chair next to her. Placing his hand over hers, he said, "Remember when we were their age? Going to the ball with our parents, dancing for hours."

Elena gave a small smile. "We felt so grown. We were only children."

"Yes, exactly," David said, "and we were happy. Christine deserves the same experiences. To know what it's like to feel so grown when you're so young, and to laugh and dance the night away with those she loves."

"You're right," Elena said, her eyes to her food. "It's just so hard to let go. I feel so responsible."

"I understand," David assured her. "I do too. And while it is our responsibility to keep her true heritage hidden and give her a normal childhood, we also can't forget who she is and why we are raising her. She is a queen. The blood of Michael and Anna is in those veins, and you and I both know it cannot be contained."

"I just—I go back there, every time she speaks of going to the ball. All I see is the flames. I fear it happening all over again."

"You cannot let the fear win," David said. "You must have courage. We both must."

Elena sighed deeply, gathering all of her strength, and nodded. "You're right," she said. "A ball couldn't hurt. And she does belong there."

David squeezed her hand in reassurance and smiled. "It is going to be a wonderful night."

"May it be."

~

Christine twirled in her dress, silver covered in white tulle. The skirt spun out around her legs. She lifted up to her toes on one foot, raising her leg and arms in the most graceful turn.

"You look absolutely beautiful, miss," Adela said, watching her.

Adela had been Christine's handmaid since she was a baby. She looked after her, kept her dressed and clean, made sure she was always fed and rose early to see the sunrise. Adela did not know exactly why she was pressed to take the most exceptional care of Christine, though she had her suspicions, but she obeyed without question. Christine was quite fond of her; they had become like friends, and Christine often used her as a confidant.

Christine stopped spinning in a plié before assessing herself fully in the tall mirror. Her long blond curls were neat, her face just slightly flushed, her lips pink. Adela had pinned flowers in her hair. She was ready.

"Thank you, Adela." She hugged her tight, straightened and said, "This is going to be the best night ever!"

Adela laughed. "I should hope so, my lady. A girl's first ball is something she never forgets."

Christine turned back to the mirror, looking herself up and down. She took a deep breath. "Adela, can I tell you a secret?"

"Yes, my lady," Adela said, folding up her used clothes and putting items away.

"When I am of age, I am going to find a prince and woo him," she near-whispered with an innocent giggle.

"That you should, my lady," Adela said. "A girl like you is meant for a crown."

"When I'm grown," Christine continued, "and can do what I want, I will travel the whole world. I'll go to every ball and learn the secrets beyond these walls."

"That sounds very ambitious," Adela said. "And could be dangerous for a lady. Would you take your brother?"

Christine scoffed. "Jack has no sense of what the world has to offer. He'll stay here forever and die an old boring man."

"My lady," Adela scolded, "you should not say such things about your own brother."

There was a knock at the door. Adela opened to see David. "Good evening, sir," she said with a curtsy.

"Adela, is my daughter ready?" David asked.

She grinned. "More than ready." She opened the door fully, stepping aside to let David enter.

Christine was standing there, hands clasped behind her back, her body swaying back and forth in excitement as she waited for her father's assessment.

"You look beautiful, Christine," David said.

"Thank you, Father," Christine glowed. "I'm so excited! I can't wait."

"Well then, we shouldn't waste any more time, should we?" David said, offering her his arm.

Christine circled her arm under his and let him lead her out the door.

"Have an amazing time," Adela called behind her.

"Thank you, Adela!" Christine turned back to say, "I'll tell you everything in the morning."

"I'm counting on it," Adela waved as David and Christine were lost around the corner.

Chapter Six

The Queen's Dance

As they made their way down the hall, Christine asked, "Father, what about Mother? Is she coming?"

"No," David said, his eyes not meeting hers. "No, I'm afraid she is staying in tonight."

"But why?" Christine urged. "Does it bother her that much that I would want to go to a ball?"

David led Christine out to a nearby balcony. The sky was a dark blue, studded with crystal stars like diamonds. Despite the late hour, there was hustle and bustle below, carriages pulling up, men offering hands to beautiful women adorned in rich clothes and jewels. The courtyard and castle were lit up and garlanded with flowers—daffodils and violets, yellow crocuses and cherry blossoms—heightening the feeling of festivity and spring.

When they reached the edge of the balcony, David stopped and turned to look at Christine, taking her small hands in his.

"Oh no," Christine said, "that bad?"

"Christine," David began, barely looking at her as he tried to choose his words carefully. No matter how old she may feel, she was still only a child and not ready for the truth of her past, her family and who she was. "A long time ago, before you were born, your mother had a very bad experience at a ball much like this one. The details are not important, but the point is, she is scarred and only trying to protect you by keeping you away."

Christine looked at her flat silver shoes, a small pang of guilt in her stomach. "I'm sorry, Father. I did not know."

"Hey," David said, lifting her chin. "It's not your fault; that's why I supported you in going and looking after you. I'm just trying to help you understand why it is hard for your mother. She understands, too, and has agreed to your attendance. It's not easy for her, though."

"I understand," Christine said assuredly.

"Good," David squeezed her hand. "Now, let's go have fun at your first ball, shall we?"

"Yes, sir!" Christine's spirit was full again, excitement growing in her stomach. She took David's arm again, and they continued to the ballroom. With every step, it grew harder for Christine to not leap with uncontainable glee. When they reached the entrance, Christine's heart began pounding rapidly. She saw women in gowns and pearls, men in handsome suits and gloved hands. Joining the flow, David and Christine stepped through the huge doors of the ballroom, and Christine's heart stopped completely. She thought for a moment that she might faint, but she didn't. Her eyes were wide, surveying the massive room to take in everything.

They were at the top of the stairs on a balcony. The stairs were wide, edged with pearl, curving out towards the bottom like the train of a dress. Hundreds of people mingled, drinking fine golden champagne filled with dancing bubbles and tiny iced cakes—one bite each—that servers in fancy uniform carried on trays. All around the room was every flower you could think of. Pinks, whites and purples of every shade, all freshly picked, filled the room with the most glorious aromas.

And then Christine's eyes found the dance floor in the middle. It was crowded with men and women dancing together, some young children in the corner also, holding hands and spinning in circles. Not a single unhappy face could be found. Christine was ready to join them.

At the opposite end of the room were three thrones, molded from gold and upholstered in dark blue velvet. They sat on a stage, two steps off the floor, a wide blue carpet draped down the front. King Luke, Queen Tara, and Prince Thomas sat on the thrones; Robert and Daniel sat in smaller ornate chairs beside Thomas. Crowns sat atop all of their perfectly styled hair. The men wore clothes of white with gold trim, while Queen Tara wore a light green gown with a full tulle skirt, flowers woven around the top of the bodice. Her shoulders were left bare. A sash of flowers circled her waist.

Fruits picked straight off the vine, breads sweet and savory brought fresh through the kitchen doors every minute, and deer, rabbits and game birds that had been hunted over the last few days filled the long tables, piled high. Fresh-caught fish in bright sauces lay beside venison pies and roasted ducks stuffed with raisins, bread crumbs and wild mushrooms. And in the rear left corner were many chairs and small tables for people to sit, eat and entertain. There was a tall pink marble fountain with fresh, clear water cascading near the middle of the room. A small girl sat beside it, dipping her fingers into its cool water.

Christine thought she had just walked into heaven itself. She looked up at David who was looking back at her with a sparkle in his eye and a knowing smile on his lips. "What do you think?" he asked.

She was breathless. "It's the most incredible thing I have seen in my whole life."

David laughed a little, remembering—remembering too much and trying not to. An ache swelling in his heart. From behind them, they heard the deep, loud voice of the man announcing guests, "Sir David and Lady Christine."

David winked at Christine, and they walked down the steps. Christine could not stop looking this way and that, seeing a man in a light blue suit ask a lady in yellow to dance, an elder lady by the table drinking wine and stuffing her small clutch full of pastries, a man kissing a lady's hand and offering her wine, and a lady coming up behind her husband and covering his eyes, a knowing smile on his face. Everywhere she turned she saw wonder and joy. She was falling in love with it all.

"Sir David," a tall, plump man in a uniform that was at least a size too small greeted them when they reached the bottom of the stairs.

"Colonel Rayn," David greeted, shaking the man's hand. "It is good to see you, sir."

"Same to you, sir," Colonel Rayn replied. "You look well. Where is your wife this night?"

"She is already seeing herself to sleep," David told him in the professional voice he only used around officers and advisors. "But my daughter Christine has accompanied me." He turned to Christine. "Christine, this is Colonel Rayn; Colonel, my daughter, Christine."

Bending to reach her, Colonel Rayn took her hand and kissed it. "An absolute pleasure to meet you, little lady," he said.

"Nice to meet you, Colonel," Christine replied with a blush, suddenly feeling so small amongst the crowd of grownups.

"Always a pleasure to see you," David said, bowing his head and taking his leave.

This went on for a while. Dukes and duchesses, ladies of wealth and men of high station all laughing, drinking and gossiping with one another about things they heard, things they saw, and some things they were sure were not true, but they sounded too delightfully sinful not to speak of.

Finally, David turned to Christine and said, "My daughter, may I have the honor of the first dance?" He bent at the waist, offering his gloved hand.

Christine suddenly glowed, accepting her father's outstretched hand and following him to the crowded floor. He had to slouch to meet her, wrapping her protectively into him before beginning to turn.

"Thank you for bringing me, Father," she told him. "This is amazing."

"It is my honor, Christine," he told her. And she would never understand how much he meant it, to be dancing at the first real ball for Christine, Queen of Dancé.

The music seeped into Christine, enlivening her body. She felt every limb twitch, begging to take flight. But she contained herself, following her father's gentle sways and turns. Even so, she felt as close to heaven as she ever had.

As the song came to an end, there was a tap on David's shoulder. Christine's eyes rose; there standing before them was Prince Thomas.

Seeing Thomas, David bowed immediately. "Prince Thomas," he said, "so good to have you back home, sir."

"It is good to be back, David," Thomas replied, "just in time for this magnificent ball." He gestured around him. "I wondered if I may ask for the honor of the next dance with Lady Christine?"

David's arm jerked a little with a sudden need to protect Christine. But then he reminded himself of who she really was and that she should be dancing with princes and kings. Even at a young age, Dancé royals would steal everyone's hearts with the glorious dances they performed and shared. Yes, this was a necessary element in preparing her for her future. He knew it, and Thomas knew it. Caring for Christine was a personal mission of both these men, David as he raised her and Thomas as he worked tirelessly with his men to restore her throne.

Even with the knowledge of his duty, there was another thing holding him back. He was not oblivious that when he was dancing Christine she had wanted to do more. He didn't think she even noticed her legs kicking out behind her, begging her to just let go. And if she did, it would be the most amazing thing this castle had seen since her mother's last visit twelve years earlier. People might start asking questions. She was ten and fragile. No matter how headstrong she felt, she was not ready to know everything—or anything—of where she came from. Not yet.

Still, David served both Thomas and Christine (even if Christine didn't realize), and so he bowed in submission to Prince Thomas. "Of course, Your Majesty." When he rose, he gave him a look of warning, hoping Thomas would see and understand to be careful.

Christine, the young queen of Dancé, practically leaped on point to Thomas, Prince of Hanton and his outstretched arm. She blushed a sweet pink, looking up at Thomas, so tall above her.

He knelt down in front of her, as he had done so many times in the past. "Hey, little lady," he said, "may I have this dance?"

"Yes, Prince Thomas," Christine breathed out, realizing how nervous she was, her hands shaking just a little.

Nervous because of Prince Thomas? No, he had been there since she was a baby, checking in every time he came home from his long trips. He was a prince, but he had been such a friend to her, especially protective of her, which she did not quite understand, but it made her feel safe when he was home. She knew Thomas, and she felt braver around him.

What made her nervous was what she knew she was about to do. She had felt her body's plea to let loose when she danced with her father. She knew that with Thomas she could release whatever it was. The thought frightened her a little but excited her too.

Thomas dipped his hand to take hers, the other properly behind his back. She held her skirt as they walked onto the dance floor. She realized that everyone else had left the floor and was watching them. This made her heart pound, but she took a deep breath, refusing to run in fear, and turned with Prince Thomas into position.

What happened next was a thing of legend; the moment the music sounded its first note, Christine's body seemed to wake from a long slumber. Thomas moved quickly to keep up with every turn, every leap, every graceful kick and sway. He lifted her at her waist, her body weightless, flying high in her dance.

Those watching could do nothing but stand in awe. Some whispered to each other, "She's only ten? Where did she learn that?"

"I've never seen anything like it." "Isn't that the daughter of Sir David?" "What is happening?"

Many were just amazed. Others were skeptical as if some trick were being played. There were some, at least one or two, who felt something deep in their gut, who knew much more was happening. They wouldn't say it aloud; they barely dared to think it, but a part of them knew that there could only be one explanation.

On the nearest sidelines, David watched, not quite in horror, but in great fear. He knew she'd be good; he knew it would draw attention, but this was so much more than he'd imagined. She was her mother the queen, just a head shorter.

Christine twirled, leaped, bent and then spun around so fast, a flower flew from her hair. At the sound of the last chord, right on key, she fell into a perfect split, hands grasping Thomas's above her head, looking out at the crowd with a smile on her face, catching her breath. In an instant, the crowd was in an uproar of claps and cheers. Thomas pulled Christine straight up, back to her feet, and they hugged each other.

"You were wonderful!" Thomas said, glowing with pride.

"Thank you," Christine beamed. "That was amazing."

The crowd began to press in on them, but David beat them to her. "Christine," he whispered loudly to be heard above the crowd in her ear, "you need to come with me immediately."

"David—" Thomas began, but David cut him off.

"Thank you for a wonderful time, Your Majesty," he bowed. "I need to get my daughter home."

Christine looked up at him, confused. Everything had just gone from perfect to—she wasn't sure what. But she had never seen her father so stern and—could that be fear in his eyes?

As David pulled Christine away, Thomas saw the flower that had fallen from Christine's hair. It was a royal purple in full bloom. He smiled at how perfect that was, the color of her flag. He carefully picked it up.

From behind him one of the uniformed officers said, "Prince Thomas." He had cut through the crowd of those pressing to fawn over him. "The king requests your audience. Immediately."

Thomas looked past the crowd to see that only his mother still sat watching the festivities. His father had disappeared. Taking a deep breath and offering proper thanks to all of the compliments thrown at him, he followed the officer to the edge of the room and slipped through the door beside the thrones.

It all happened too fast for Christine to question or object; she just followed her father—not that she had a choice, he would not release her hand—out of the ballroom through a side door. They began to walk the halls back to her room.

"Father," Christine questioned. "Father, please. What is wrong?"

David could not respond. His head was racing too quickly; he couldn't even hear her until they reached the door to her room.

"Father, please," she said again as they finally came to a stop.

Coming back to the moment, David realized he was squeezing Christine's hand much more tightly than he'd meant to.

"I'm sorry," he startled, quickly releasing her hand.

"Father," Christine said again, "did I do something wrong? Are you upset with me?"

David took her face in his hands. "No, my child," he said, searching his brain for the right words. "I could never be upset with you. I just—something urgent came up." He let go of her. "I'm sorry, you must turn in for the night."

Christine looked at him with so much confusion. She did not understand what was happening. So she did as he instructed and went into her room where Adela was waiting for her.

Adela rose to her feet as Christine walked in. "My lady, you're back earlier than I expected."

Christine just stared straight at nothing, brow furrowed.

"Lady Christine," Adela asked in concern, "is everything alright? How was the ball?"

"It was—" Christine tried to speak. "It was perfect and then—" She looked straight at Adela. "I don't know what just happened."

Chapter Seven

The Queen in Hiding

David marched down the hall, trying not to draw attention, but his pace was faster than normal. He was clearly on a mission. He reached the king's study and was let in immediately by the guards standing outside.

Thomas was bending forward over his father's desk in extreme frustration, saying, "It is not her fault; the blood of Dancé courses through her veins. It's who she is!"

"And that is precisely why you should have known better than to ask her to dance with you!" the king rebutted. Both men were angry, both rightfully so.

"David," Luke said, seeing he had entered. "Where is Christine now?"

"She is in her room," he told the king. "She is—confused. I was not sure what to tell her." David hung his head, feeling overwhelmed and shamed at his aggressiveness with Christine. They all just wanted the best for her, but it was growing harder to see exactly what that should look like.

"I do not see what the problem is," Thomas continued as if not hearing anyone. "So she has dance in her veins. She should be allowed to dance and be who she is. She is a queen! Blast, she is the Queen of Dancé!"

"And she has been in hiding here for ten years now with no questions or suspicion," the king spat back, "until the moment you asked that young girl to dance. Now people are asking. If not asking, they are wondering. Thank heavens her legs were covered; if that birthmark—" he stopped, unable to say more. He turned to the window, a frustrated hand jerking through his hair.

"So what if she is discovered?" Thomas asked. "I know when she was a baby it made sense, but now?"

"She is not ready," David said. "She acts old, but the girl is still a child. She is trying to grow too fast, and perhaps in fear of not raising the Queen of Dancé properly, I'm giving her too much freedom. I should not have let her come tonight."

"It's not just that," King Luke said, turning back with a deep breath, trying to calm himself. "She didn't lose her parents to natural causes; they were murdered and her entire kingdom destroyed. We don't know by whom—even though we have sent out investigators and questioned everyone we can think of. They covered their tracks too well! We don't know if the murderers are sitting by to see if an heir appears. You want to risk the life of a small child to find out? The last of her line? Do you want to be the one to tell that innocent child, who is always off dreaming, that this isn't her home and that her parents have both been dead almost her whole life?"

Thomas looked down at his father's words. He knew he was right and that it was too soon to expose Christine in that way. That did not change the fact that keeping the secret was wearing on him.

"I'm sorry, My King," Thomas said. "You are right that she is innocent, though she would do her best to make you believe she is at least sixteen. She is only a child and needs more time. But for almost every day of the last ten years I have worked, hands-on with my men, as we rebuilt her kingdom. And to come home to that high-spirited child who seems to be waiting expectantly for me to be finished, though I know she is utterly unaware. Restoring her to her throne has become my mission. I may have been wrong, but God, to see her dance like that. It was like nothing had ever happened, like her mother and father were there. That dance was her birthright."

"I understand your feelings," David said. "And for a moment, I too felt that way. Everything was as it should be. But she is not ready. And as the king said, we are not certain yet if it is even safe."

Luke took a seat behind his desk, folded his hands in front of him and addressed both David and Thomas. "There is no way to avoid the fact that this happened. So I will spread word, and I will expect you both to as well, that Christine has been tutored in dance since she could walk. After all, her supposed parents are from Dancé, so she could legitimately have dance in her blood. We can say this is how David and Elena are honoring their homeland. And we will do whatever we can to make this whole thing seem less than it was.

David, try to keep Christine out of the streets and away from too many prying nobles for the next few days. The less she knows about the questions, the better."

"Yes, Your Majesty," David bowed, accepting his orders.

"Thomas," Luke continued, "you have a very special connection to Christine, and I understand that the work you do contributes to that. For now, I think it best you return to Dancé, just until the questions die down. And when you return, try not to be as attentive to Christine. Do not let her think you are angry, or she is not worthy. But back away as much as you can. It is for her own good."

Thomas's fists were clenched on the desk as he leaned his whole body into them, knuckles growing white and jaw set. He was angry. He made no effort to hide it, but there was also nothing he could say now that the king had spoken.

"As you command, My King," Thomas said through gritted teeth.

He turned and went to the door, jerking it open. Before leaving, he turned back to say, "You may be right, but this isn't."

With that, he was gone.

"He is right, you know," Luke said once the door was slammed shut. "It is not right, but we can't change it. I don't know if this has ever happened before. An heir hiding in a neighboring kingdom, waiting for the day she can go home. What do you think?"

David sat in the chair across from the king, relaxing into it with a sigh. "I think," he began slowly, being very careful with his words, "that there is no right answer here. I believe that all we can do is our best and pray to God that in the end, it all turns out right."

Luke nodded in agreement. "My son is angry with me."

"I think we are all angry for the situation, not at anyone in particular. Well—maybe the ones who put us into this situation by destroying the most beautiful, noble couple, my homeland—" He choked up.

"All these years later and I still do not understand why anyone would have wanted to burn such a kingdom, so full of life and kindness, straight to the ground," Luke said sadly.

"I do not know. But I believe that sometimes anger turns to hate, and if it consumes you, the last thing you want to see is others' happiness," David said. "I don't think the people that did this hated Dancé and its people as much as they hated themselves."

The king nodded. "You are wise, my friend. Go, look after Christine, keep her out of sight for a few days until this chaos passes."

David stood and bowed. "Yes, Your Majesty."

David left the room, and Luke stood to look out the window again, his hand pressed against the frame. The night was black, diamond stars shining above. He was taken back to the night they released lanterns in memory of all those lost in the massacre of Dancé.

In his mind's eye he saw them, rising from the ground as far as the eye could see.

Then he recalled the day King Michael told him that his wife was with child. The glow of overflowing happiness in his eyes; "I'm going to be a father!"

Luke and Michael had been close. They'd known each other since they were boys, only princes, reckless and full of ideas. He could not wait to meet his friend's firstborn, but he could never have imagined that when he did, it would follow the devastating loss of his best friend. He knew Michael would have wanted Luke to look after his daughter's wellbeing by any means possible. And he trusted David as well, a man who had never left his side and only concerned himself with the king's best interest. They were both doing the best they knew to do. But was it enough?

~

When David returned to his room, Elena was still awake, sitting in her chair by the fire reading a leather-bound book. She sat up straight when the door creaked open, closing her book. She looked at David expectantly, but his eyes would not meet hers as he stripped off his coat and began to loosen his collar.

"David?" Elena asked, concern filling her voice.

David sat at the end of the bed, his elbows to his thighs as he rubbed two large hands down his face.

Elena got up from her chair and moved over to him, kneeling on the ground beside him, her hands on his legs, looking up at him so he was forced to look down at her. "David?"

David's hands were fisted in front of his mouth, but he stared back at her.

"I don't know what to feel," David admitted. "She was—perfect. She danced beautifully, just like her mother. It was right in every way, and I have never seen her so happy and free. She was truly herself."

"But?" Elena asked, knowing it was coming.

"But—she was truly herself; the Queen of Dancé," he sighed, "she was too exposed. The king and I have met, and we have to keep her out of sight for a few days until the questions die down. Prince Thomas has been sent back to Dancé for a while."

"The prince?" she asked, confused.

"Yes," David said. "He was the one who danced with her."

"Why?"

"Because just like us," David said, "he knows who she is. And just like we want to give her the best childhood, he wants her to be honored as the queen she is. We are all too close to this whole situation."

Elena was unsure of what to make of all this. She had known Christine going to the ball was a bad idea. But she thought her fear was an irrational one that the enemy would be present, would attack.

She had not thought that it would come down to Christine just being herself—and an irresistible subject of rumor.

"So what do we do now?" Elena asked.

"I am not certain," David said, "but we have to keep her out of sight for a while. Perhaps give her a little more structure."

"She has been avoiding her tutor," Elena said. "And Tilda is anxious to begin lessons to help her be more of a lady in preparation for her future."

"Making her focus on those things could be just what needs to be done," David admitted. "It is just the right thing, not punishment but something to keep her too busy and distracted to make herself obvious."

"I will talk to them first thing in the morning to set it up," Elena said, "and we will let Christine know too."

David placed his hands over his wife's and looked into her eyes. "Thank you," he told her sincerely.

She smiled back at him with a bow of her head, and that settled it.

~

When Thomas left his father's office, his hands were still clenched and his face red from his outburst. Making his way down the hall, he found the glassworker Gavin. He was in the cellar where he worked. The room was hot, the air tinted red from the fire.

Gavin was a very dirty man. Soot and sweat smeared his face, clothes and strong arms. His hands were holding a long pole that dipped into the hot furnace, spinning it slowly to shape. Pulling it from the fire, he rubbed the side of the burning glass with a thick cloth, turning it and forming the orange glowing glass into ripples. Thomas stood and watched him work, heating and turning, forming and cutting. Finally, he put the glass vase he had just completed in a secure cabinet to cool.

"You do incredible work," Thomas said.

Gavin looked up, realizing the prince was there. "My Prince," he smiled broadly, "it has been a while since my lair has been blessed with your presence. To what do I owe this pleasure?"

Thomas held out the delicate purple flower that had fallen from Christine's hair during the ball. "I want this sealed for the ballroom of Dancé. Make it just right to be sealed into a wall. Please."

Gavin took his gloves off and reached out with a clean hand to take the flower from Thomas. He let it lie in his hand, inspecting it. "It can be done," Gavin said. "I can start working on it right away while the flower is fresh. I can have it ready for you in the morning."

"I won't be here in the morning," Thomas told him. "If you would save it for me until my return, I would be in your debt."

Gavin bowed. "Whatever you wish, My Prince."

"Unless it is me or one of my men, do not show it to anyone."

"It is done," Gavin assured him.

Thomas had plans for the small flower. It would be sealed into the wall of the ballroom. Even after Christine was gone, her memory and the memory of her parents would live on forever, for all the generations of royals that ever hold the throne to see.

That night, by the king's command, Thomas and his men departed Dancé without another word to anyone. By the time the people of Hanton woke, they were gone again, and all speculation gradually died down.

~

The next morning Adela found Christine in the garden. Christine thought the garden was the most beautiful place in all of Hanton. Adela often found her there reading, picking flowers or just sitting in the green grass dreaming. The garden was large, the sunrise edging everything in gold. Flowers of every kind and color lined the paths and the walls and were scattered among the grass. Vines wrapped around the white gate with beautiful morning glories coming into bloom. In the middle of the garden was a round stone floor, wide enough to have a large party, as had been done in the past. Four benches sat around the circle, allowing you to sit and enjoy the air, birds' songs and the smell of spring. In the middle of the circle was a fountain of white stone. The sound of rushing water joining the birds' song.

This morning Christine was not reading or dreaming; she was dancing. From one side of the circle to the next, over the benches and around the path. Adela stood and watched her, smiling at her freedom and amazed at what she could do.

When Christine finally spotted her, she stopped in an instant. "I didn't see you there."

"I didn't mean to startle you," Adela said. "You were doing so well and looked so happy, I didn't want to interrupt."

Christine dropped her head, her hands folded in front of her. "I danced last night. At the ball. Now Father is angry with me, and I don't understand it. He's never been angry with me before."

"He could never be angry with you," Adela said, taking a seat on one of the benches. Christine slumped over with her.

"All I did was dance. I've never done it before, it just—happened," Christine said.

"I don't know why your father makes the choices that he makes," Adela admitted, "but I know it is always with your best interest at heart. You are very valuable to him."

Christine thought for a minute. "He's always treated me like his little girl," Christine agreed. "But last night—I don't know what happened, everything was perfect, and then it wasn't. Adela, I've never seen him like that. And he tried to tell me that 'something just came up,' but I know better. I could see his eyes."

"Even when we don't understand it, there is always a reason or explanation behind everything," Adela said. "Trust me, my lady. It will all make sense in time."

Christine turned straight in her chair and looked at a small flower she had plucked, twirling it in her hand. "Adela?"

"Yes, my lady?"

"Do you ever feel like you don't belong?" Christine asked. "Like you're somehow different from everybody else?"

"I think every person goes through that when they are young," Adela told her. "As you try to grow from your parents' child to your own person, find out who you really are, everyone has some period when they feel they just don't fit into the puzzle."

"It's more than that," Christine said. "I know they love me, but sometimes—it's how they look at me. I share ideas, dreams, and Mother and Father, they look scared. And Jack, he just thinks I'm a silly simpleton."

"Well, all brothers are like that," Adela laughed.

"I don't even look like my family," Christine continued, paying Adela's words no mind. "My hair, my face—"

It was true. Christine had white-blond curls that were thick and soft. But David, Elena and even Jack all had dark brown hair. Her face was also longer and her nose smaller with a dainty point. Her eyes perfect almonds. Adela could not deny the obvious differences. But her job was to care for the girl in every way, so she said, "Perhaps you had a grandmother you look more like. I look more like my grandmother than I do my own mother."

"You're probably right," Christine sighed, deciding to let it go. She still didn't feel right, and it would still bother her. But continuing to talk about it was getting her nowhere. No one understood how she felt. Perhaps no one could.

Over the next months, Christine saw her freedom chipped away. Instead of spending days running free with her brother, she was sent to tutors who schooled her and more importantly, taught her how to be a proper lady. David saw this as a good excuse to keep her away from the crowds while also preparing her for her future as queen. Elena agreed with this, though she never forgot the ball and dreaded what its effect might eventually be. They all tried to move past it.

At night, Christine would still sneak out her window, climb down the wall by the crate and vine until she reached the grass. Then she would run as fast as she could until she reached the tree she and Jack used to sit on every day. She'd perch herself on the branch, looking out at the world that seemed to never end. She could not help but dream and wonder what was beyond those green hills. She determined that one day when she was old enough, she would find out.

Chapter Eight

Runaway Queen

8 Years Later

As the years went by, Christine felt more like an alien in Hanton. She was tutored to the point of excellence in math, reading, and language. The only thing she was not taught was geography. David did not want her to know just yet what country lay to the south. She was tirelessly put through etiquette classes and even dance. The dance was her father's idea. She thought it was ridiculous since she danced better than any of her teachers, but David saw it as a way to hopefully explain her skill.

Christine was alone. She didn't have any friends and was kept too busy to hang around her brother much, though she was closer to him than anyone else. They would steal away to the tree sometimes and talk of life and the future. She had not been permitted to go to another ball since she was ten. After how the last time ended, she quit arguing and did what was asked of her. Even Thomas, who had always been a friend to her, was very distant. He was kind, but no longer friendly. Where once he bent to his knee, now he offered a mere tilt of the head, which left Christine feeling small.

Christine's birthday was only a week away, which meant everything would soon be revealed. She would finally understand the mystery of her life, and the queen would sit on the throne of Dancé once more. David, King Luke, Prince Thomas, Captain Stephen and General Reed were gathered in a private room to decide how everything would be accomplished.

"A ball," General Reed plainly announced, as if it was the only logical option. "We shall have a grand ball where the queen shall be presented before everyone, and there she will receive her crown."

The crown sat in the middle of the room on a stand. It glistened in the light, diamonds and emeralds on every side. It was Queen Anna's crown, the one found after the fire. It had been cleaned and restored to its original beauty. Two diamonds had been added to the front in honor of Michael and Anna.

"We should tell her first," David said, "privately. Her life has already been a confusion for her. She will need time to process everything before we throw a ball and crown at her."

"I agree with David," Thomas said.

"It is only proper for a queen to have a ball on her eighteenth birthday," General Reed demanded. "Perhaps we can tell her now? Get it over with and be on with the rest."

"She may be queen," David said, "but she is still just a girl about to have her whole life turned inside out. Everything she's ever known revealed as a ruse. We cannot be careless about this. We must tread lightly and think before we say anything."

"Lightly," Reed scoffed. "She is a grown woman now. Were she a man, we would not bother ourselves with feelings. And to that, if she cannot handle the truth, she cannot handle the crown."

"That is not up to you, General," King Luke said finally. "Whether *you* like it or not, that girl is the rightful queen of the throne of Dancé. Prince Thomas and his men have been working for eighteen years, clearing and constructing an entire kingdom. Eighteen years, and we are to tell an innocent child that her whole life has been a dance around the truth. That her parents aren't her parents, that they actually died when she was born. David and Thomas are right, and you damn well better listen and watch your step here, sir."

"You wanted my opinion on the matter," Reed said simply, throwing up his hands in defense. "I have given it."

Just then there was a knock at the door, and one of the guards entered, his eyes wide with fear. "I beg your pardon, Majesty. It was urgent."

"Well, out with it then," Luke said with exasperation.

"Sir David," the man said, redirecting his attention, "it's Lady Elena. She fell in the garden, sir. It doesn't look good."

"Your Majesty?" David asked.

"Go, David," Luke said with a wave of his hand, "see to your wife. We will have to put all this on hold for now. Not one of you is to say a word or make a move until I say so, or it will be your head."

David bowed to Luke before racing off to find Elena and see what was wrong.

~

Elena was lying in her bed, gasping for air, her body hot with an uncontrollable fever that made her skin bright red. Jack and Christine were on either side of her, holding her hands with deep concern on their faces. Christine was crying, "Mother, please—"

David burst through the door, breath quick from his sprint. "Elena!" He hurried over to the bed, Jack stepping back to give him space. Falling to his knees in front of the bed, he grabbed her weak hand in both of his, tears immediately threatening him. "Elena, I'm here. It is alright." He looked up at Christine and Jack, who was now walking up behind her. The doctor stood in the corner putting away his instruments. "What happened?"

"One of the servants found her fallen in the garden like this," Jack said, his face wide in fear. "They called the doctor immediately. She's getting worse by the second."

"Sir," the doctor said in a calm, low voice, "may I speak with you outside for a moment?"

David looked at Elena, her eyes closed, her body struggling to hang on. "I'll be right back," he promised her.

David followed the doctor out to the hall. The doctor kept his calm, quiet voice as he spoke discreetly to David. "Sir, your wife seems to have a terrible infection. Though I am not sure what has

95

caused it, I have seen these symptoms before, and it only ends one way."

The doctor paused. David's whole body was shaking with fear and rage. "Damn it, man. Tell me!"

The doctor looked into David's eyes with all the sympathy he could muster. "No one has ever survived, sir."

David began to hyperventilate, tears falling from his eyes. He covered his face and fell against the wall. His legs gave out, and he slid down to the floor weeping uncontrollably. Elena had been in seemingly perfect health. She was still so young. How could this happen?

The doctor squatted down beside David, putting a gentle hand on his shoulder and said, "Sir, I know this is an impossible situation. Your wife needs you now, your children need you. The best thing you can do right now is to be with her. Hold her hand, let her know that you're not leaving. Don't let her think you are so upset, or she will not be able to let go, and her suffering will increase."

The doctor gave David a handkerchief, which he accepted, wiping his face clean. His eyes were red; there was no way to hide it. But with a few deep breaths, he pulled himself together enough to face Elena. The doctor offered his hand to help David back to his feet, which he accepted. Without any words, he nodded to the doctor and then made his way back into his room where his wife lay dying.

Christine's face was tear-stained. Jack sat next to her with a vacant stare. His whole body numb.

"She's burning up," Jack said to David when he walked in.

"Is she going to be alright?" Christine asked.

David walked over to the stool on the other side of their bed. When he took Elena's hand, she opened her eyes just barely to look at him. He smiled as best as he could, and her eyes closed weakly.

Jack and Christine were both looking at him in expectation. Taking a deep breath, he said, "Remember that time, it was late at night and your mother wanted cake? But being the person she is, she refused to wake the cook."

"So she decided to make it herself," Jack said.

"Chef Cookie was so mad the next day when he found she had messed with the kitchen," Christine laughed through tears.

"She did it though," David said. "She made that cake."

"It was the worst cake I've ever tasted," Jack giggled.

A weak tug on Elena's mouth let David know she was aware of their presence.

"Yes," David said looking at her. "She was so upset. And when Cookie found out, he baked her the perfect cake."

"It was the best cake I've ever eaten," Christine said.

"And big enough to feed half the castle," Jack added.

"Your mother always has a way of making people adore her, no matter how ridiculous her quests," David finished.

Elena's grip pulled at his hand just slightly, and he squeezed back.

"Father?" Christine asked in a near whisper.

David looked up at her and saw the concern mingled with the question in her eyes. He shook his head in answer. Christine understood, nodding and trying to keep her fresh tears silent.

"I'm sorry for all the grief I caused, Mother," she said. "I know you were always just looking out for me, even when I didn't understand it."

"You are always there," Jack said. "No matter what, you always stick by us."

"You are always and forever my greatest love," David whispered.

And that is how they remained, sharing stories, sitting together and embracing every last moment.

~

Late that night, Elena's body gave out completely, and she died. Cries of anguish filled the room as the world suddenly stopped for the small family.

The funeral was the next day. It was a gathering of her closest friends and family. Luke and Tara came as well to show their respects to David and the children. There was an unspoken decision that anything having to do with Dancé and Christine would have to be put on hold until the time for mourning had passed. A queen should not start her reign in black.

Jack was inconsolable to the point of angry. He locked himself in his room, unwilling to open for food, drink or even Christine, who sat outside his door for hours at a time. He would yell through the door for anyone who knocked to just leave him alone.

David became distant from everyone, hiding away to mourn. He showed up for meals, but he would look no one in the eye. It was obvious he was trying to be there, but he wasn't. He'd pick at untouched food, answer questions with a single word and then disappear again, nothing but wine on his stomach. No one was exactly sure where he went, just that he would not be found until he was ready.

Christine felt numb. She'd cried her tears when Elena died, but she was ready to not feel anymore. She needed something to focus her mind on, but there was no one to help. So she spent hours in the studio, dancing alone. Her mind was lost in memories. With every turn, she began to dream, pictures of a better world filling her mind. One where people did not die, where she was known and loved. A world that didn't make her feel so foreign.

Five days passed, and nothing had changed. Christine was sitting in the library one day reading one of her favorite books when she overheard two girls whispering together.

"You know they say they're not even her parents?" the first one said.

"Who?" the second asked.

"The daughter of the dead woman—Christine, I think."

Christine felt a pang in her heart. She wanted to confront the girls who were probably her age, but she was frozen by their words.

"Where did you hear such a story?" the second girl asked.

"I heard my father whispering something about it to the king. I didn't hear much, but her parents are dead. Everyone is lying."

"I wonder who she really is then. Perhaps they killed her parents."

"Don't be so dark!"

Christine filled with panic, she felt like her heart was going to explode from inside her chest and the walls closed in around her. All her nightmares seemed to be coming true, and she had no one to turn to, nothing to do but run—and she did.

Tears in her eyes, gasping for air, she ran as fast as she could to find her father. He wasn't in the garden, or the study. Finally, she found him in his room, crouched on the ground in the corner. He had Elena's ring in his hand, turning it in circles, watching its light flash as it hit the light. An almost empty bottle of wine was in his other hand; he didn't even bother with a glass anymore. His eyes were vacant, almost like a dead man.

"Father?" Christine beckoned his attention with an ache in her gut.

"Leave me," David said without looking up.

"Is it true?" She pressed, too anxious to leave without an answer. "You aren't my father. My parents are dead?"

At these words, David's eyes were pulled from his trance. His brain was a fog, but he knew he heard her right. This reaction was enough to send the feeling of a stake through Christine's heart. "Where did you hear this?" David asked, trying to pull himself to his feet. He stumbled before reaching his knees, and fell on his shoulder. A tinge of red wine spilled on the floor.

"Does it matter?" Christine asked, "If it were a lie, you would have denied by now."

Tears were now flooding from Christine's eyes and David pulled himself back to sitting, with a nearby chair as his support.

"Christine—no—it's not what you think—" David stumbled through words, trying to pull back Christine's attention. "Please, I—I cannot explain it all to you now." He pressed a hand to his head, a headache like a dagger beating at him. "I—you—Christine, you have to trust me. Everything will make sense soon."

Christine's eyes were now a vacant stare into the distance, she felt as though she had been killed and her insides were now hollow. The pain too great to even be pain anymore. "You are not my father."

"Christine," David pleaded, "give me until tomorrow. I swear to you; I will explain everything then. Please."

Christine took a shaky breath, and without another word, left David alone. She returned to her room and sat in the window looking out at the evening sky. The last rays of sun tinted it in purple and orange, like a canvas painted by a great artist. Christine just stared at it, without thought, without feeling.

Then her mind began to race, playing back her life. Her childhood days were filled with games and laugher, she and Jack always together. Jack—was he even her brother? Still, it was a time of freedom and joy. She remembered the night where everything changed, the night of the first and last ball. The night she danced with the prince and magic filled her bones. The years following were just lessons, school and an entirely different atmosphere. She was still hurt by the way Prince Thomas had looked at her on his short visits home, that beloved face courteous but blank before he turned away. All the magic that had consumed them both forgotten. Her family, now mere acquaintances.

A day from eighteen, what she thought would be the best time of her life, and everything had collapsed on top of her. She didn't know who she was, who her family was, if anything in her life was ever real.

Her hands fisted in her skirt, breath quickening as possibilities began to build in her head. She could leave. Pack a bag, take her horse and find out what was beyond those hills. She could have that adventure she'd always dreamed of. No one could stop her. With her mother gone—or the woman she knew as her mother—nothing was holding her here. She had Jack and David, but she and Jack had grown apart when her life became so confused and proper. She knew he loved her and she loved him, but she was grown now, and it was time to find her own place in the world. And her father—oh, she was close to her father—but he wasn't her father. What she felt as betrayal made her heart feel a coldness to him.

She didn't have roots, plans, hopes for a future. She was floating through life, hoping for something miraculous to happen. Perhaps it was time to make it happen for herself.

All her life, she had dreamed of adventure. Any time she spoke of travel, her father had always shut her down. He would never allow her to leave Hanton. For some reason, everyone wanted to keep her caged. She just wanted to *go*. Before her, she saw an open door. Beyond it was the unknown, the unexplored, her dreams in reality. It was thrilling and frightening. It was now or never.

Filled with a new sense of purpose, she rose from her seat and began to pack a bag. Just a few small items she would need, nothing more. When her bag was full, she sat at her desk and wrote a letter.

Dear Jack,

I fear you may not understand, but I have to go. I love you dearly, but there is nothing left for me here. I need to find myself, who I am, my place in this world. While I will miss the days we ran free as children and sat for hours, dreaming in the tall oak tree—we both know those days have been gone for years and will never be given back to us. Perhaps one day you will see me again. I will return with my Prince and a babe in my arm. Until then, I wish you all the best.

And tell father…

She paused for a moment, quill extended above the page. She wanted to say she was sorry, but the feeling of betrayal would not let her even write the words. She wanted to say she loved him, but she didn't even know who he was anymore.

~~And tell father…~~

I will miss you both. I love you, Jack.

Your beloved,

Christine

She sealed the letter and left it on her desk. Then wrapped a long black cloak around her shoulders, covering her head with the oversized hood. She moved to her windowsill where she sat for a moment, looking back into her room. Her heart was racing; she was really doing this. One day she would return, but not until she had seen the world, and perhaps found a place to belong.

Tearing her eyes away, she moved out into the cool night air. Her shaking hand grasped the cool vine she had used so many times to sneak out. With a frightened certainty, she began her descent. When she reached the ground, a new rush of determination filled her. Already, she felt herself coming to life.

She snuck around to the kitchen. It was dark and deathly quiet, everyone gone to bed. She filled a second bag with food, apples and water. Then she went to the barn where she found her horse Knight. David had given her the horse when she was a girl. She loved that horse, tall and strong. Riding him always made her feel older and in control.

She rubbed her hand gently down the side of his long face and soft neck, whispering, "Hey, boy, you ready to go on an adventure?"

Knight jerked his head up and gave a high "Neigh."

"Good boy."

Christine saddled Knight, secured her bags on him and lit a lantern. "Ready, boy? Let's go." She grabbed the reins, pushed her heel into his side, and they were off. Leaving the barn at a trot, she put a little distance between her and the castle, then began to race.

The night air rushed against her cruelly, but the cloak Christine wore was enough to keep her warm. The wind on her face as they rode only spurred her on. A sense of freedom rushed over her. Skirt flying in the wind, hair in a loose bounce behind her.

Racing for the hills she had stared at far too long, they ran. Today was the day she would learn what was beyond them. She rode until she found herself riding up an incline. Knight's pace slowed a little, but he did not stop until they reached the top of the first hill. When they did, they both looked back and saw Hanton, a small glow sticking out into the night. It looked tiny from where she sat, and the perspective hit her hard. The little world, all she had ever known, a speck on a canvas. Finally, she turned the other way to see the world she had only dreamed of. Mountains followed by plains seemed to go on forever before turning into thick woods.

She patted the side of Knight's neck. "No turning back now, boy."

They were off again, disappearing into the night.

~

Jack woke the next morning feeling worn and weak. He wrapped himself in a robe, feeling he had just enough strength to eat. Jack opened the door. It was the first time he'd seen anything beyond his four walls in days. The hall looked empty and foreign, but a man stood by, likely placed there by his father or sister.

"Would you have the cook fix me some breakfast?" he asked.

The man nodded, "Yes sir, right away."

As the man ran for food, Jack returned to his room and waited.

When the chef was informed Jack was ready to eat, he moved swiftly into action. "It is about time that boy ate something," he grumbled, flipping red ham on the grill and scrambling some eggs. "A day longer, there would be nothing left to feed."

Within thirty minutes, a maid was entering Jack's room with a tray of food. Hot eggs, a fresh biscuit, tender ham and some freshly cut fruit were all laid on a tray before him. A cup of tea with lemon was also served. The aroma was strong in Jack's nose. He thanked the maid and turned all his attention to the meal.

Jack's hands were weak and shaking as he reached for the biscuit. Pulling off a small piece, he put it in his mouth and closed his eyes. The bread was soft and warm, freshly baked. Food had never tasted so good. His body soaked up every bite, slowly reclaiming some of its strength. He took a sip of the tea, its temperature just right. It went smoothly down his throat and warmed his stomach. Losing his mother had almost been too much for him, but he was ready to live again, even if his life would always have an emptiness at its core.

When he finished eating, a warm bath was drawn for him. He took his time washing, embracing the warmth of the water and the scented soap on his skin. As he washed, he felt himself cleansing away the last days, all the heartache. It would never go away, but the pain broke just enough for him to move forward.

Once he was dry and dressed, he decided he would go and see his sister. He knew she had been neglected, heard her soft cries outside his door when he was too numb to answer. He was ready to make it right. Walking down the halls, he made it to her door and knocked.

"I think she is still sleeping, sir," Adela told him quietly. "She hasn't called on me all morning."

"Does she usually sleep this late?" Jack asked.

"No, sir," Adela admitted, "not for a long time. Perhaps though, the passing of the Lady Elena has been too much for her."

Jack didn't quite like the feeling that gave him, so he knocked again, this time much louder. "Christine, answer me. It's Jack. I'm sorry I've been so distant—I would like to see you. Please open the door."

Silence.

"Christine, I'm coming in!" Jack called a warning before going to open the door. It jiggled but wouldn't turn. Locked.

"She never locks it, sir," Adela said, concern becoming clear on her face.

Jack tried pushing harder, but the door wouldn't budge. Moving back, he rammed his shoulder into the door. The frame broke from the bolt, and pain radiated from his shoulder. He didn't think about it though, pushing past to see that Christine was gone. The bed had not been slept in, her chair by the window was cold, and her closet stood open.

"She may have gone to the tree," Jack said, hurrying past Adela.

He raced down the hall, unwilling to acknowledge what was already clear. He ran until he saw the tree, standing alone, tall and green. No girl hid amongst its branches.

Jack's heart thumped. Panic was quickly setting in. "Christine!" he called out, cupping hands around his mouth. "Christine! Where are you? Christine!"

No answer.

He ran back to the castle, his legs faster this time, whole body in a panic. Reaching his father's room, he beat on the door. "Father! Father, open. Now!"

David reached the door in moments. "Jack?" he asked. "What is the meaning of this outburst?"

"Christine," he gasped. "She's gone."

David looked confused, then realized what Jack had said. His eyes grew wide in terror. Memory of their short outburst the night before making him sick. David ran past Jack, who was right on his heels, returning to Christine's room. David came to a stop in the middle of her floor, frozen. He saw the room was empty, barely touched in a day at least. He looked in the closet and saw her cloak gone. "She said nothing to you?" he demanded of Adela. "She is not visiting anyone?"

"No, sir. She went to bed as usual....and then nothing. I waited outside her room all morning."

"Father."

David turned to see Jack standing in front of Christine's desk, a small piece of paper in his hand. David moved beside him and they both read silently. With every word, David's whole life, his purpose, what he worked for, his mission—he feared complete failure.

"I must see the king," David said. "Wait here."

"The king?" Jack asked, not understanding how that would be the next logical step. "I am coming with you."

"No, Jack," David said, turning and holding his hand up. "You must wait here."

"She is my sister!" Jack retorted. "I am coming with you."

David sighed. Jack was now seventeen, old enough to know responsibility. And perhaps even to keep the biggest secret of his life. Either way, he did not have time to stand and argue with him. "Fine," he said, "but we must hurry."

David and Jack raced through the halls and up another flight of stairs before coming to the king's office. Two men stood guard outside.

"I must speak with the king," David said.

"I am sorry, sir," one of the men replied. "He is not to be disturbed right now."

"Disturb him!" David yelled. "This is of the greatest urgency. I must see the king now."

The two men looked at each other, a little taken aback. One of them went to the king. "Your Majesty, I apologize. It is Sir David; he demands to see you immediately. Says it's of the utmost importance."

"Let him in," Luke instructed.

David entered, Jack right behind him. Luke was sitting behind his desk, Thomas across from him. Thomas had that angry look on his face that had seemed permanent the last few years. They had definitely interrupted something and were only about to make it worse.

"Your Majesty." David and Jack both bowed to King Luke and then Prince Thomas.

The men nodded back before David continued. "Christine is missing."

Thomas rose from his chair immediately. "What? How long? Are you sure of this?"

"I don't think so." David explained. "She is not in her room and no one has seen her since last night. Additionally—"

"I even went out to the tree Christine likes. She was not there either," Jack told them. "And then I found this on her desk."

Jack handed the note to Prince Thomas who accepted it with anxious hands and read every word like a spy looking for clues.

"Guard!" Luke called. He had heard enough.

When the man entered again, he said, "Send Captain Stephen to me immediately. Tell him we will need a search party."

The young man bowed his head and was out the door, carrying out the king's demand.

"Where was she last seen?" Luke asked, returning his attention to David.

"According to her maid, when she went to her room for the night," David told him.

"If she ran away in the night, she could be anywhere," Thomas said in dismay.

"Pondering will not help us," the king said. "Thomas, you will take your men and go north. I will take a group south. David, you will lead men to the east, and I will have Stephen lead men west. Every group is given a week to search before returning here to regroup. And pray to God that we find her, or she returns home. Or the Dancé bloodline is gone forever. There will be no restoring it."

"We will find her, Your Majesty," David said. "We have to."

"I will ride with you, Father," Jack said.

"You must stay—"

"No!" Jack didn't even let him finish. "She is just as much my responsibility as yours now. I will not just sit here and wait for news. I'm coming with you."

There was no arguing with Jack, and he knew it. "Fine," David conceded. "But you do not leave my side, not once."

"Yes sir," Jack agreed.

Stephen entered at that moment, "Majesty," he said with a bow, "I was told there is to be a search. Who are we looking for?"

"Christine seems to have vanished in the night," Luke told him. "We have to find her."

Stephen's horror suddenly mirrored that of the rest of them. They immediately set to work. Luke sent word to Tara of what was happening and that she must take care of everything in his absence. Within the hour, twenty of the king's horses were racing from the gates of Hanton, groups of five in each direction in search of the runaway queen.

The king's words were sticking in Jack's mind: "The last of the Dancé bloodline." What did he mean? Jack was desperate to ask his father, but it would have to wait. For now, it was a race and a prayer one of them would find her.

Before it was too late.

Chapter Nine

Search for the Queen

Christine had ridden all night long. She'd found a path in the forest, so she had followed it. Since it was her first time leaving Hanton, clearly marked roads seemed her friends. She stopped to let Knight rest, fed him a couple of apples and gave him water.

"There you go, boy," she cooed. "You are riding well."

He rubbed the side of her arm with his long face. She giggled and wrapped herself around his neck. They had a close connection ever since she was young, and she loved it.

So far, she had seen woods, grass, and even more trees. It was beautiful, no doubt. But it wasn't what she had expected when starting this grand adventure. In the books she read, she had found descriptions of distant cities and towns that offered different people, foods, and experiences. She didn't have much sense of how far away such places were, or what directions they were in. She wasn't aware that this was a deliberate omission in her education; it had just never seemed important. She was not giving up yet, though; her journey had only just started.

When Knight was rested, she mounted him once more, and they were off. They rode half of the day, through paths in the woods, across great plains and rolling hills. The path she took seemed well traveled, which was a sort of comfort to her. She thought of Prince Thomas, all the times he would disappear on his adventures. She wondered if he had taken this path. She had asked him about where he went, as a little girl, but he would just tell her silly stories about talking birds and trees that had fruit all year round. Then, when she was older, they hardly ever spoke. Still something about this path felt familiar to her. She felt an unexplainable comfort.

When the sun was at its highest, she could finally see something very far off in the distance. An ocean, long and vast, stretching as far as the eye could see. She paused for a moment, taking it in. She had never seen the ocean before, though she had read many books that described its beauty and majesty.

Then something caught her eye far to the left. Perched near the ocean was a kingdom, much smaller than the one she came from, though it seemed to glisten under the sun. She did not see anyone outside, but she decided to take a closer look. Spurring Knight on, they rode for the unknown city.

As it came closer to her view, the roar of the ocean grew louder. The sound of the waves crashing on the shore was music to her ears. It was wild and peaceful. She had ever heard a more magnificent sound and the sun sparkling on the waves made her want to dance.

The city was made of white and grey stones. The walls were high, and deep purple flags snapped in the wind. Gold thread was sewn into the flag, depicting a rose wrapped in thorn and vine. It was beautiful but far too quiet. The gates were sealed shut; it was a little eerie. With not a soul in sight, she thought it best to continue on. Turning, she began to follow the line of the ocean. The smell of salt in the air tickled her nose. The continuous cry of the waves was making it hard to stay on the horse.

When she had moved beyond sight of the abandoned kingdom, she and Knight stopped again. After giving him food and water, she removed his saddle, and secured his reins to a tree. Then she fastened her skirt on either side of her waist, exposing her knees. Leaving her boots and bag with Knight, she made her way to the ocean.

With bare feet, she walked through the sand, loving the feel of it between her toes. She went slowly, turning her foot and curling her toes, feeling the way it moved and crumbled underfoot. When a cold wave raced up the sand and touched the tip of her toes, she jumped back in surprise and then giggled with childlike glee. Moving forward again, she stepped into the wave, inhaling deeply as the cool water splashed to her ankles. As the wave returned to the sea, it took the sand from under her feet. She wobbled and moved, feeling very uneasy and a little frightened.

Eventually, she got used to the waves and the sand, walking out as far as her knees. She splashed her hands in the water, making the sea her friend. She spun and danced with the waves, kicking her leg to create a splash and spinning through the wet sand. Knight lay in the nearby grass, resting and watching her. She felt like a little girl, happy and free.

When she had her fill of play, she went and leaned against the tree next to Knight. Resting her head back, she closed her eyes, soaking the sun into her wet skin. Soon, she was asleep.

Hours later, Christine woke with a fright to the sound of a thunderclap. Sitting up, fully alert, she saw that it was now dark. Knight was standing beside her looking out at the brewing storm. Lightning forked in the sky in sudden blazes, making the trees around them glow like terrifying black figures. Christine was in a panic. She had seen plenty of storms, but all from the safety of the castle. Out here with no shelter, she was shivering with cold and fear.

She rose to her feet, wrapping her cloak around her body and saddling Knight. She was desperate to find shelter before the rain began to fall. She snapped the reins, and Knight took off in a sprint down the coast. Realizing she needed to find higher ground, she turned and rode away from the beach, deep into the woods. She had to slow, the dark night making it almost impossible to navigate the trees, no longer following a traveled path.

She saw nothing but woods and black. Not even a hint of light in the distance from a lantern. Nothing. For the first time since leaving Hanton, she was unpleasantly aware of her solitude and wished Prince Thomas was here to guide her. The thunder continued to crack the sky, the strikes of lightning giving her glimpses of her surroundings. The wind had picked up tremendously, making her very cold.

Finally, she noticed a small cave up ahead, just big enough for her and Knight if he laid down. It was a place to hide in until the storm passed. She dismounted and led Knight, encouraging him to bend low and creep in with her. Slowly, he was able to take the space next to her. They curled into each other for warmth. She wrapped her cloak tightly around her, saying a prayer that they would survive whatever the night might bring.

Minutes later, the sky began to fall upon them in sheets of water. The cave was small enough that the hard rain drove into them, and the ground beneath became wet. Christine leaned close into the warmth of Knight, his long neck across her lap.

"It's going to be alright, boy," she told Knight in an effort to soothe herself.

The night was long, the rain relentless, and air only grew colder. Christine remained wrapped as well as she could, her cloak covering her from head to toe, her body keeping in heat next to Knight's soft fur. She tried to sleep, but every new thunderclap jolted her back. She began to wonder if they would survive the night.

~

Although Prince Thomas had wanted to take the route to Dancé, arguing that he was most familiar with it, David ended up convincing him that he should go. He was hoping that something in her blood had drawn Christine there, that he would find her where she belonged, in her own kingdom.

They made it to Dancé not long after the rain began to fall. Seeing his homeland clothed in darkness under pouring rain gave him a painful heartache. He longed for Elena.

"We should stop until it passes," one of the knights told David.

"No," David demanded. "She could be out there. I am not stopping."

"Sir," the knight persuaded, "the horses are tired, the rain a cascade, and it is dark. If we continue on now, we could pass six feet from her and still miss her. We must stop."

David could not deny they had run the horses hard. They, as well as the men, needed a rest. So against every bone within him, he conceded.

"As soon as the storm passes, we continue on," David ordered.

"Yes sir," the knight agreed.

David stopped to look at Dancé, not very far in the distance. It looked dark and glum in the storm. He hadn't the strength to return to Dancé since that tragic night eighteen years ago. It was his hope to return with Christine on her eighteenth birthday. That didn't seem very likely now, but he still hoped.

The five men who had been riding together made it to Dancé and entered the empty castle for shelter. Thomas and his men had done well rebuilding. When they walked through the front doors, David's heart skipped a beat. He felt as though he had gone back in time, as if all he needed to do was race down the hall and Michael, Anna and Elena would be there to greet him. A futile dream. The silence of the castle was almost frightening. Every footstep echoed off the walls like a ghost.

The horses were sheltered and fed, and the men found food in the kitchen, which had been placed there for the unveiling ball. They ate, quaffed goblets of wine and found a room full of cots. They stripped their heavy armor and looked for comfort in sleep.

David however, could not sleep. Neither could Jack, but David did not know that. At the sound of snoring from the men around him, David rose quietly from his cot in the corner and crept out of the room.

The rain was beating hard against the roof, a low rumble within the safety of the castle walls. David worried about Christine out there in the storm. Guilt from the last time they had spoke was beating at him. Perhaps if he hadn't been drinking so much—if his head had been clearer—if he had handled the situation better—maybe she would be safely in the walls of Hanton. He wanted to continue his search; his body would not rest from the need, but he knew the men were right. The horses could only be pushed so far. Not to mention, finding anything in this dark storm would take a miracle.

David shook his head and balled his fists. How had they come this close only to lose Elena and Christine within days? He knew she was a free spirit, and the rules of the castle were wearing on her. He kicked himself for not realizing it had gotten this bad, not understanding how the death of Elena would affect her. She was unsettled and desperate, and he had only made the situation worse.

David wandered until he found the new royal chambers, placed almost perfectly where the old ones had been. He quit breathing when he opened the door and saw the room. It was just like before, only without a carriage in the center of the room. The tall golden bed was draped in purple sheets, the high chest and solid dresser topped with gold and crystal figures. Michael's sword David had taken the night of the fire had been placed on a stand, his name etched in the blade. Candlesticks holding candles yet to be lit rested on the windowsills. Looking at the untouched wicks, the image of Dancé in flames flashed through his mind. He closed his eyes, wishing it away and walked over to the large window. Placing his hands on the wide sill, he squinted his eyes in an effort to see the ocean through the pouring rain. Though the storm was a roar, the ocean roared louder, assuring David it was still there. Its strong waves were on a constant journey to reach the castle walls, though it would never succeed.

"Father?"

The low, soft voice from behind David startled him. He spun around to see Jack standing in the doorway, a solemn look on his face.

"Jack," David replied in a surprised whisper. "What are you doing in here?"

"I followed you," Jack admitted.

David sighed. He should have known that Jack would not stand by and wait. He was David's son after all.

"You've been here before," Jack said, more as a statement than a question. It was clear David knew the castle. Still, Jack wanted his father's confession. He was also hoping for an explanation for everything bizarre that had happened since Christine's disappearance.

David took a deep breath, summoning all of his strength. "Come," he said, extending his hand in invitation. Jack followed David to two high backed chairs in the corner.

Jack realized this was the first time he and his father had spoken since his mother's death. It seemed weeks ago now, though she was yet only a thought away. He sat stiffly in one of the handsome chairs padded in velvet. David sat next to him, hands shaking.

"Does this have something to do with Christine?" Jack asked impatiently.

David leaned his elbows to his knees and looked out into the room rather than at Jack. "Yes," he finally admitted. "Everything leads back to this place—and Christine. Your mother told me she was pregnant with you in this very room. Well," he corrected himself, "the room that was here before."

"I don't understand."

"It is a long story," David said.

"The storm is not letting up anytime soon," Jack observed with a wave of his hand. "I would say we have time."

David nodded. "I will tell you, Jack. But you must understand that everything I say has been secret for your entire life. Unless given permission by myself or His Majesty, you must never breathe a word of this. Not even to Christine when we find her."

"The king knows?" Jack asks. The more he heard, the more questions he had.

"Jack," David said firmly, "you must promise me."

"I promise,"' Jack assured him.

Looking at the floor, David gathered his thoughts.

"Your mother and I were both born here," David began. "So were our parents and grandparents before us. This kingdom was a place that was legendary. You had to see it with your own eyes to believe it was real. Until the day it became legend through destruction. What made Dancé special was the royal family. There were things that seemed impossible. Every king was wise and every queen gracious. But there was much more to it. Every child born with royal blood had an immediate ability to dance. Without lessons. It was just something that was inside them, like the ability to walk or talk. Not only was it natural, it was beyond what the greatest ballerina could ever do. Just to watch them, you would be lifted into another world. A world where anything was possible. And it was through this that everyone else claimed their own magic, believing in themselves and making the impossible possible.

"There was another thing. Just like the color of hair or eyes, a marking was on every royal from birth. A rose, like a birthmark but clearly shaped, on the outer left ankle. Boy or girl, they were all born with it."

Jack's forehead wrinkled. "Christine has a mark like what you speak of. It looks just like a rose on her ankle."

David inhaled and continued, "When Christine was born, a celebration was to be held. During this celebration, Dancé was overrun by unknown enemies. Every person within the kingdom was killed that night. The castle and every home burned to the ground. The only survivors were me, your mother, who had just found out she was pregnant with you, and Christine."

"Father," Jack started, "you can't be saying—"

"Christine is not your sister, Jack," David blurted while he still had the strength. "She is the only remaining heir to Dancé."

Jack gaped at his father, who wouldn't meet his eye. Everything he had known his entire life, a lie. His own sister not his sister. Rather, a royal? Why had they kept this from him?

"This is impossible," Jack said. "Christine, she is just a girl. My sister, the one who ran with me, climbed trees and wrestled in the grass. You are saying she is not my sister; she is actually a princess of some—lost kingdom?"

"A queen," David corrected.

"Does Christine know?" Jack questioned.

"No," David confessed. "It has been a secret since the massacre. We were going to tell her within days—perhaps we waited too long."

"Christine always felt different," Jack said, thinking over his childhood with Christine. "She talked often about how she didn't belong and how she wanted to see the world. She wanted to 'find herself.' I just thought she was a silly girl. Why was this kept from me? From her, knowing how she felt?"

"Perhaps we waited too long," David repeated. "We spoke of it often, but the timing was never right. She was too young to understand; Thomas was still building. Additionally, we didn't know who destroyed Dancé, or whether they were still out there for many years. It wasn't until a couple years ago, King Luke and his men discovered the men who destroyed Dancé and brought them to justice. That is why the truth was kept a secret for so long."

"You give her little credit," Jack objected, agitation growing. "Christine is strong; she could have handled the truth. And are you telling me that those 'long trips' Prince Thomas would take—he came here? He did all this?" He gestured around the room.

"Yes."

"Father, how could you keep this from us?"

"I was trying to do what was right," David said, his voice rising. Standing, he began to pace. "There is no handbook 'How to Raise an Orphan Queen.' We could only do our best. It was not perfect, our decision, but it was with Christine and Dancé's future in mind. Your mother and I watched the place go up in flames, with no way to stop them, no way to save any others. Can you imagine that? All our family, friends, our king and queen. We had been instructed to watch Christine; she was our main responsibility. So we did what the king and queen would have wanted. When we were ambushed, your mother and I got their daughter out. We thought they would escape, meet us in Hanton. But after finding refuge, no one joined us. We were the only ones who made it out alive. There are no words for the sorrow we felt.

"We sought the council of King Luke. He took us in, and we made a plan. When Christine turned eighteen, we would tell her everything. By that time, Thomas would be done with rebuilding, and we would return Christine to the throne. It is her birthright."

"A lot of good that did," Jack said. "Now she is gone. She didn't understand her life, so she is gone."

David leaned against the wall and slid down to the floor. "I had one job, to protect the Queen of Dancé and return her home. One job, and I failed."

David looked out into the dark room, focused on nothing. If he had lost Christine forever, then what good was his life in the end? Had he been too hard on her? Did he not give her enough rein or was the truth held from her too long? There was no way to know for sure. What he did know was that every friend and family member he had known growing up was lost. He had been left with three, and now his wife had been taken from him as well, and Christine was nowhere to be found.

Jack felt terrible for what his father had lived through, but he was also angry. If only he had known sooner, perhaps he could have taken better care, or at least kept a closer eye on Christine. Understanding now how real her feelings were and how lost she was, his heart was breaking.

"So what now?" Jack asked.

"We find her," David said, "We find her, or we never stop looking."

~

The rain finally subsided at dawn, giving way to a clear morning sky. Birds chirped, awakening from the long night and flying here and there to find breakfast. Knight nudged the side of his head closer to Christine whose arms were still wrapped around him. Her head lay settled on his neck as though he were a pillow, and she was sleeping softly.

At Knight's nudge, Christine stirred awake. She blinked a little, trying to remember where she was. Her clothes were soaked, and she sat in a pool of water. She groaned unhappily, digging into one of the sacks on Knight's back in search of food for the horse. He chewed happily on an apple she offered him as she rubbed his back and surveyed their surroundings. The trees around them were tall and covered in green leaves. Unlike how it had seemed at night, the forest was very beautiful and full of life. The sun crept through leaves of every shade of green, and squirrels raced up and down the tree trunks. A blue morning sky was above her. She felt the warmth of the sun.

Nudging Knight, she pulled herself to her feet, muscles aching from the position she had slept in. Knight rose and stood beside her. There was no way of knowing where they were, where they had come from or what direction they should ride. Everywhere she turned there were trees. No sign of path or sea.

She dug in one of the bags, finding some clothes that had been protected and stayed dry. It felt awkward changing outside, naked and exposed to the air. Quickly as she could, she stripped off all of her wet clothes and replaced them with dry ones. The sun felt warm on her skin, drying and comforting her. Once she was dressed, she took Knight's reins, and they began to walk together. She did not know where they were going, her sense of direction lost; they just walked.

It felt good to walk, to stretch her legs and take in everything around her. The bird's song was a continuous chorus, and now and then they would startle a deer, which would bound away on swift legs, or a rabbit would dash across their path. Christine loved it; seeing all the life and freedom lifted her spirits. She wondered about David and Jack. She knew they would be worried; she felt a little guilty. But her feeling of betrayal overshadowed it. For now, her adventure was all that mattered. She would not return until she was satisfied.

After a couple of hours, she found a well-trod path in the woods. She mounted Knight and continued on. That afternoon, when the sun was at its highest, she heard the sound of running water. They found a stream nearby and stopped to drink and wash up a little. After that, they continued on until nightfall.

This went on for three days, every day Christine expecting to come across a town or at least a house. But there was nothing but forest. She ran out of food. She and Knight were both tired from the journey. Christine's clothes were covered in dust from riding, her hair a tangled mess. Even her face was covered in loose dirt, kicked up while riding. Her eyes drooped, and her stomach ached. If they did not find food and water soon, she feared she would die.

She wondered if it would have been better to stay in Hanton. Had she made a mistake leaving without plan or direction?

Knight rode at a slow pace until Christine grew so weak, she fell off the horse's back to the ground, hitting her head on a rock, which knocked her out cold.

Knight stopped, dipping his head to nudge her face. When she didn't respond, he laid his large body next to hers and went to sleep.

~

After four more days of riding, David and the group with him had reached the point of exhaustion. They had been through three towns, spoken with everyone that would listen. No one had seen a girl matching Christine's description.

"She's lucky if the elements haven't killed her by now," one of the knights said.

"She is alive," David spoke angrily. "I can feel it in my bones."

"We have to go back," the knight urged. "His Majesty gave us a week. If we haven't found her by now, we aren't going to."

They sat on their horses atop a high mountain. David was looking out over the rocky valleys below. He was sure Christine would not have come this way. He knew in his heart they would not find her, though he would never admit it aloud. As hard as he pushed, expecting to see Christine's blond hair flying in the wind ahead of them, he knew she was gone. All he could do now was pray she would have her fill of adventure, stay alive, and return home one day soon.

David finally conceded, and they turned back to Hanton.

As they rode, Jack asked, "She will come back, won't she?"

"If God wills it, it shall be done," David said, unsure of anything.

"Perhaps one of the others found her," Jack said, trying to give his father hope.

"May it be," David agreed.

Two days later, they made it back to Dancé. They were worn, dirty, and their hearts were heavy. Stephen, Luke, and Thomas all returned as well, and no one had caught even a glimpse of the runaway queen.

"She could be anywhere," Stephen told them. "At this point, she is a small needle within a stack of hay."

"She will come back," Thomas said. "She has to come back."

Chapter Ten

The Queen's Adventure

Captain Matthew of Reigland was a fine man. He was taller than most, his hair a light brown that shagged in loose ripples down his neck. His eyes were hazel and shone like gold in the sun. His body was fit and strong from years of training and battle. His presence was commanding, but his heart was gentle.

He was out riding with eight of his men, scouting the countryside and hunting game. Their horses galloped loudly, kicking up dirt from beneath green grass. They rode over hills and through trees, taking in the day. As they reached the top of a small hill, Matthew halted his men with the raise of a hand. "Whoa!" he called to men and horse.

Every horse stopped immediately to see what had caught Matthew's eye. A black horse lay on the ground as though dead. A small arm and near-white blonde hair lay across the grass beside it.

"Captain," one of the men said, "it looks like a maiden."

The man who had spoken, Troy, was tall, though he did not reach Matthew's height, and his body was strong. His hair was black like a raven's feathers. He was skilled in archery, and his eyes could see for miles.

"Dead most likely," another man said.

"Keep a lookout," Matthew instructed. "There may be raiders."

With that, Captain Matthew and his men rode down the hill heading straight for the horse and its lady. As they approached, they could see it was a frail woman who looked more dead than asleep. The men circled around her, and Matthew dismounted, bending down next to the girl to check for a pulse. When he did, the horse's eyes lifted slightly to look at him.

"Give this horse water," he commanded, removing his gloves to better assess the woman.

She was the most beautiful woman he had ever seen, lean and pale, though her skin was pink from the sun. Her eyes were closed, her face peaceful. Her hair spread around her shoulders like a white blanket. She was angelic.

Matthew touched her head. Her skin was warm, a good sign. Rolling her onto her back, he saw dried blood on her face and hair. He noted the rock her head had been laying on, also stained with blood, and knew she must have fallen on it. Still, she was not dead; her chest rose and fell with breath.

"Water," Matthew commanded with an outstretched hand, his eyes never leaving the woman, his other hand supporting her head.

A flask of water was placed in his hand within seconds. He poured some over her head to clean it. He was able to see she had a large gash, but that was it. He knew their doctor would be able to help.

"Lady," he said gently to the sleeping angel, "can you hear me? Wake up."

All the men were staring down in silence, waiting to see her stir. Even Knight, who had been given water now, was looking down at Christine in expectation.

A slight groan left her lips, and she lifted a weak hand to touch her throbbing head.

"Don't," Matthew told her gently, moving her hand before she could touch the wound.

Her eyes fluttered slowly open, confused and trying to figure out where she was and who was holding her.

"Drink," Matthew said, putting water to her lips.

At the taste of water, Christine finally moved to pull it closer. She drank like a woman who hadn't drunk in days, which was true. When she had drunk the entire thing, she opened her eyes and looked up. She wondered for a moment if David and Jack had found her, but the eyes she was looking into were golden, the face younger than her father's and older than her brother's. The man was handsome, and Christine thought she must be dreaming.

"I'm Matthew," the kind man with the handsome face said. "What is your name?"

"Christine," she told him weakly.

"Where are you from? Do you know how you got here?"

Christine rubbed her forehead. Her memory was so fogged; she honestly could not remember anything beyond her name.

"I—I don't remember," she said. "Where I am?"

"You are in Reigland," Matthew told her, "and you are safe. You've been hurt, but we will take you to a doctor."

Christine moved her eyes around to see all the men on horses above her. So many closed in, they almost blocked out the sun.

"These are my men," Matthew said. "They will protect you. I'm going to carry you to my horse."

Matthew put his arms under Christine and lifted her from the ground, her small body like a feather in his arms. She wrapped her arms around his neck, feeling secure within his grasp. He put her on the back of his horse and then mounted behind her.

"Troy, take the horse to the stables, make sure it is fed and given water," Matthew ordered. "And have him looked at. He is weak, so be patient with him."

"Yes, Captain," Troy nodded.

"Bleeker, Wallace, ride with him. Go at the pace of the horse," he finished.

"His name is Knight," Christine whispered weakly, her head leaning against Matthew's chest, eyes closed.

"Knight," Matthew told the men. "Be gentle with him. The rest of you, ride with me. We will hurry back to the city and I will get her to the doctor."

Not wasting any more time, Matthew snapped his reins and was off, most of his men riding behind. Troy and the two with him were feeding Knight food from their sacks and giving him water before they rode.

Matthew was brisk, while keeping in mind the fragile woman in his arms. She was leaning against his strong body for balance, her fingers gripping the mane of his horse. Matthew wondered where she had come from. She seemed like an angel fallen from heaven. All that mattered now was getting her to the doctor.

They rode hard until they reached Reigland. The walls and towers were built of grey stone. Thick iron gates screeched an awful sound as they opened to let the riders in. The road was dirt, beaten hard from being ridden on every day. The streets were busy with maids and farmers roaming markets, and high-class ladies gossiping from under colorful parasols. Many ladies looked at Matthew riding in and blushed at the handsome captain. Others whispered to their friends, giggling of impure fantasies. Matthew didn't pay them any mind, worried only for the woman with him.

Christine peered through heavy eyes to see the flag of Reigland. It was black as night, with blood red stitching depicting a fierce, fire-breathing dragon. The look of it almost gave her a shiver. Everything here seemed dark and frightening compared to the color and life of Hanton. But then she remembered the eyes of her rescuer, the one holding her steady against him. Those were not eyes of a sinister man. They were eyes with sincerity and honor.

As they rode further, she saw children playing in the streets, a happy game of tag. They stopped at the sight of the king's men, faces bright with excitement as they waved to the soldiers. Christine smiled, relaxing a little at the sight.

Matthew didn't slow until they came to a large white mansion, with pillars lining the front balcony. It looked like the home a duke would live in. Coming to a stop, Matthew dismounted his horse before pulling Christine into his arms and carrying her inside. Again, she wrapped her arms around his neck, resting her head on his hard chest. His cloak was soft on her cheek, and she inhaled the smell of it.

"Kendal, tie up my horse and make for the castle. Tell the king what happened," Matthew ordered. "I will see to the lady."

Kendal nodded to the captain and moved to carry out his demands. Matthew turned to the home, his long legs taking the steps two at a time.

"Isabell!" he called as soon as he entered the front door.

Henry, Isabell's husband, came rushing around the corner at the sound of Matthew's desperate call. Henry was a man of average build, his face kind and gentle. Dark brown hair was pulled into a ponytail at the nape of his neck. He wore brown trousers and a white shirt with his sleeves rolled to his elbows.

"Matthew," Henry said in surprise at the sight of Matthew carrying a lady.

"She needs medical attention," Matthew explained urgently. "Where is Isabell?"

"She is upstairs with a patient," Henry said, his feet already moving to the winding steps. "Bring her; there is a room open."

Matthew followed Henry up the stairs. There were many doorways down the long hall in either direction. Henry didn't hesitate, leading Matthew to an open door at the end of the hall. As they passed the room where Isabell was caring for a patient, Henry stopped to tell her, "We need you."

"I'll be there in a moment," Isabell called back, her voice soft and gentle.

When they made it to the room, Matthew laid Christine down on the clean bed. The room was small and sterile, a single chair next to the small bed, a wash pan and small chest of drawers containing medical items. A single window on the wall welcomed the sunlight and a view of the blue sky outside. Christine's eyes wanted to pull shut, but she kept them open long enough to survey the room.

"Get her some water to drink," Henry instructed, getting a wet towel to clean the dried blood from Christine's head. She hissed in a breath at the pain.

"I'm sorry, love," the kind man said. "We've got to get it clean; don't want to lose you to infection, do we? It would be a shame to lose a pretty lady like you to something silly like that."

Christine smiled a little through gritted teeth, pressing her eyes shut. A large hand wrapped into hers. Without hesitation she squeezed on it tightly, tears falling from her eyes.

Henry stopped, satisfied with his work. "Don't cry, love, it will all be alright."

The strong hand left Christine's, and she felt her head being lifted.

"Drink," she heard Matthew say and felt the cup pressed to her lips.

She accepted the water to her mouth with no hesitation.

"Better give her this too," Henry said. "Something stronger to numb the pain."

A moment later Christine was drinking something awful that burned her throat, but she didn't fight it.

"Oh, you poor dear," Christine heard the soft voice of the woman say. She assumed it was Isabell. Christine opened her eyes a moment to see the woman in a burgundy dress who had just walked in. She was curvy, and tall for a lady. She had frizzy red hair that was pulled into a long braid and pale, freckled skin. She was beautiful, Christine thought, her green eyes kind like Henry's.

"What happened to her?" Isabell asked Matthew as she examined Christine's head, arms, and torso, checking for anything else broken or bruised.

"I found her in a valley outside the city," Matthew told her. "She was lying on the ground, knocked out. We thought she was dead at first, but she came to. Said her name is Christine."

Christine hissed and squealed a little when Isabell pressed her ribs. "She's got a couple of cracked ribs," Isabell said. "We'll need to get her out of these clothes and wrap them. I'm also going to stitch her head. Henry, draw a bath; she needs to be cleaned first."

Matthew waited in the room while Henry and Isabell took Christine to wash and wrap her ribs. When she was clean, wrapped and in clean clothes, they brought her back to the room. Matthew held Christine's hand as Isabell stitched her head. She quit trying to hide the tears. The pain was too much.

When Isabell was finished, Christine gave in to sleep, her body exhausted from everything.

"She is going to be alright," Isabell told Matthew who still sat beside Christine.

"What happened to her?" Matthew asked. "Can you tell?"

"I can't be certain," Isabell told him. "She is very malnourished. She has likely been wandering without food or water for at least a couple days. As for the head and ribs, it looks like she took a fall."

"There was a horse with her," Matthew informed. "Looked like she had fallen on a rock."

"Falling from a horse would do it," Isabell confirmed. "She will need lots of rest, water, and soup. It should only be a week or two before she's back to normal. Do you know where she came from? Does she have family we need to inform?"

"No," Matthew said. "She couldn't remember anything when I asked her."

"Slight amnesia is very possible following head trauma. Her memory should return, hopefully, but it could take some time."

"Do you think she could stay with you, at least until we know more?" Matthew asked.

"Of course she can stay here," Isabell said without hesitation. "It was already my intention."

"Surround me with women, my friend," Henry said. "I have no objections."

Isabell laughed and shook her head. "Don't listen to him. He wants me to bear him a daughter is what it is."

The thought of Henry and Isabell with a daughter made Matthew smile. "You wish punishment upon yourself, my friend."

"That I do," Henry confirmed, wrapping his arms around Isabell's waist.

Matthew turned his attention back to Christine who was asleep. Her face was peaceful, her hair a glorious mess around her pillow, her hand settled gently in his grasp. Isabell noticed his feeling and said, "Go home, Matthew. Wash up and then return. You are welcome to join us for dinner and check back in on your damsel."

"Keep a very close eye on her," Matthew said. "And send for me if anything should change."

"Oh, the boy is smitten already," Henry said.

"Henry, hush," Isabell scolded.

"What? You can't blame him; she practically fell from heaven into his waiting arms," Henry said.

"You find everything romantic," Isabell said, looking up at him.

"That's why you love me," he winked at her.

Matthew just looked at Christine. He knew she was safer in the hands of Henry and Isabell than she would anywhere else. Reluctantly, he pulled his hand away from Christine's, setting it gently on the bed. Then he stood.

"I will be back before nightfall," he said.

"Good, I shall be cooking my world-famous soup," Henry said gleefully. He was always happy, finding the ray of light in every darkness. It was indeed why Isabell had fallen in love with him eight years prior. And he fell for her desire to care for others. They were good friends with Matthew, having gotten to know him well after caring for him and his men. They had treated minor wounds and done their best to ease the pain of fatal ones. They had been good to

Matthew, and he felt forever in their debt—they would never see it that way though.

Matthew obeyed Isabell, going home where his servants drew a warm bath. When he was clean and dressed, he rode to the royal stables to check on Knight. Troy had made it back with him not long earlier. The stableman was looking over Knight, who had his head in a trough of fresh water.

"How is he?" Matthew asked when he approached.

"No obvious injuries," Stablemen Wilton told him. "He's just old and had been ridden without water for longer than a horse should be."

"I believe his rider was lost," Matthew told him. "She was more neglected than he."

"Well, he will be fine," Wilton said. "Some rest, food and water. And a good scrub down I would say. He will be good as new."

Matthew put his hand on Wilton's shoulder. "I do thank you."

"It's what I do, sir," he said with a shrug.

Matthew smiled and turned on his heels, making his way back to where a stable boy was holding the reins of his horse. The boy was feeding him treats and rubbing him down.

"You have him spoiled, Andy," Matthew said with a laugh.

"I'm sorry, Captain," the boy said shyly.

"Don't be," Matthew replied, rubbing the other side of his horse's long neck. "He thanks you."

The boy handed the reins back to Matthew with a nod.

"Captain!" Troy called before Matthew could mount.

"What is it, Troy?" he asked.

"How is our lost angel doing?" Troy asked.

"Hurt, but she is going to be fine. I'm headed back to see her now," Matthew told him.

"Heading back? Why, Captain, if I didn't know any better, I would say you fancied the lady. Though you don't know anything but her name and that God-sculpted face."

"I confess, that may be her appeal," Matthew said.

"Well proceed with caution," Troy warned. "A little mystery is fun until you are beaten by an angry husband."

"I shall heed your warning," Matthew said and mounted his horse. "I will see you in the morning."

"Tomorrow," Troy confirmed with a nod. And Matthew was off.

Chapter Eleven

Welcome to Reigland

When Christine woke, she didn't know where she was. Surrounded by white walls bathed in grey from the setting night, a window in the room let her see a dark world, stars glistening in the sky. The bed she lay on was firm, but soft. She was clean and wrapped in a fresh gown and warm blanket. The room was small, and when she turned to her right, she saw a man sitting beside her bed. He didn't see her at first, his eyes focused on a book in his hand. He was relaxed in the chair and clearly immersed in the story he was reading.

Slowly her fuzzy brain came back into focus. She remembered riding, exhausted and weak with hunger. She remembered stirring to the voice of a man. She remembered his face as the one who was sitting here now. Who was he? A hunter? A warrior? He carried her, she remembered now. Brought her back on his horse.

Knight! What happened to him? Remembering her horse, she began to panic. This caught Matthew's attention, so he set down his book and moved beside her.

"Shh, it's alright," he said, taking her hand.

"Knight," she spoke desperately. "My horse, what happened? Is he alright?"

"He is fine," Matthew assured her. "One of my men took him to the stables. He's been fed and looked after. He is going to be fine."

Relieved, she noticed the throb in her head and reached to touch it. Matthew caught her hand before she could. "No, you hit your head hard. Split it open. Isabell, the doctor, sewed you up. It will hurt for a few days."

Christine eased her hand back down. "Where am I?" she asked.

"You are in Reigland," he told her. "We found you beyond the border, thought you might be dead. When we saw you were hurt, we brought you back here. Your horse as well. How did you end up out there?"

Christine tried to think through the pain. "I—I was riding—I don't remember." She began to panic again and tears pricked her eyes.

"Hey, hey, it's okay," Matthew said. He rose from his seat and eased her back down to her pillow. "Isabell said you may have trouble remembering some things. Do you know where you are from?"

"No." A tear fell from Christine's eye, the feeling of loss her only lasting friend.

"You're not running away from something—someone—are you?" Matthew asked.

"No," she said. "I don't think so. Just searching for something."

"What is that?"

"I'm not sure," she told him honestly. "I guess I'll know when I find it."

He gave her a small smile. "Well, Isabell has said you are welcome to stay here as long as you want to."

"That is very kind," Christine said.

"Are you hungry?" he asked.

"Starving," she replied with a small laugh.

"If you are up to it, I think Henry's famous soup is about ready."

"That sounds wonderful, thank you." She wiped tears from her face and smiled.

Matthew offered his hands to help her sit up. Her head felt like it was being squeezed and stabbed with a knife. It made her wince, but she kept on. Once she was sitting, she pulled off the blanket and swung her legs over the side of the bed. That's when she noticed the pain in her ribs and grabbed them.

"Your ribs are not in good shape either, but they will heal soon," he assured her.

He took her hand again, and she stepped off the bed, feeling dizzy.

"You got it?" he asked.

"I'm good," she said, trying to sound stronger than she was.

Slipping her feet into the slippers Isabell had left for her, she accepted the support of his arm as they made their way to the dining room.

When they entered, Isabell was putting plates on the table. She spotted them and said, "Oh you are awake!" clapping with joy. "Henry, bring one more bowl, please!"

Henry stepped in with a pot of soup. "Well, good morning, love," he said, a welcoming smile on his face. "Glad to see you up and about."

Christine was still trying to adjust to her surroundings. She'd spent nights out in the forest, in the middle of the pouring rain, and now she was in a welcoming home with three people who had shown her kindness. It was overwhelming.

"Come in, have a seat," Isabell insisted.

Matthew pulled out a chair, and Christine settled in. A bowl of warm soup was set before her, and the aroma filled her nostrils. It smelled like heaven. She could not remember the last time she had a warm meal.

"Go on," Henry said, "you must be famished."

Without needing to be asked again, Christine dipped a spoon and took a sip of broth. It immediately warmed her, and she felt life coming back to her bones. She scooped out some of the chicken, so tender it nearly dissolved in her mouth.

"This is amazing," Christine said.

"I'm glad you like it," Isabell said.

When everyone had their fill, Henry asked Christine, "So Christine, tell us about yourself. How did you end up in our humble home half dead?"

Isabell elbowed his ribs, releasing a groan. "What he means is," Isabell said, "how are you feeling?"

"Better," Christine said. "Thanks to you. And to answer your question, I don't know. I dreamed of a castle, rich and glorious, but cold and unwelcoming."

"It could take some time for your memories to return," Isabell said softly, "Don't push yourself."

"I know I was riding," Christine said, "ran out of food, water and was lost in the middle of nowhere. Thank the Lord you found me, or I would be dead."

"Thanks indeed," Henry said playfully, eyeing Matthew.

Isabell rolled her eyes. "Don't listen to the men, Christine. It's not every day Matthew brings home a girl, and I do believe they have forgotten how to behave."

Christine smiled and said, "Tell me about all of you and this place. It is quite exciting, finding myself in an unknown place, having dinner with an unknown crowd."

"I did that once," Matthew said. "When I was a boy of fifteen, I was quite rebellious. Thought I knew everything, so I took off on my own. Found myself in Skillow, in the home of an old woman who claimed to be a witch. Come to find she was just a lonely woman who'd taken a liking to me. Came crawling home, tail tucked, within days. Father sent me to training the following morning, and here I am."

"And where is here exactly?" Christine asked.

"Captain of the king's guard," he told her.

"Yes, we've seen this boy go from a rebellious teen to a man well respected," Isabell said. "We have all been very proud of him."

"And what about you?" Christine asked Isabell and Henry.

Isabell turned sparkling eyes to Henry. "Henry and I have known each other since we were children. We used to bully each other in the schoolyard. When we grew older, Henry here thought better of himself. Went from throwing dirt at each other to bringing me flowers and poems."

"She is the most beautiful lady to ever live," Henry gleamed. "Strong, beautiful and then she went into medicine. I had to have her."

"And I wouldn't hear of it," Isabell said stubbornly. "He smiled too much, was happy over everything. No one is that happy."

"Until you realized you loved it," Henry said, taking her hand and kissing it sweetly. She blushed.

"Somehow I survive," she teased.

Christine's heart ached in the most wonderful way. They reminded her of paradise, made her believe anything was possible.

"Sounds like a fairytale from a children's book," Christine said.

Isabell laughed. "Yes, well, unlike Cinderella and Prince Charming, we do get on each other's nerves. He makes me crazy; I know I do him as well. But there is more than enough love to make up for it."

Henry and Isabell were gone, staring into each other's eyes and smiling like children who were just given cake.

"Don't mind them," Matthew whispered into her ear. "You learn to just drown out their sap."

"It's sweet," Christine replied quietly.

"Tomorrow, after you've gotten plenty of rest, I'd be glad to show you around," Matthew offered, "May even help you remember something.

Butterflies fluttered in Christine's stomach. "That would be wonderful," she replied.

And neither of them saw Henry and Isabell looking on with knowing eyes.

~

Cora, Princess of Reigland, lay across a rich couch, adorned in silk, jewels and paint. Her hair was straight, black, and fell around her shoulders. Her eyes were a piercing green, her lips thin and pursed. She was tall and thin and pointy. Her long, slender fingers, painted red at the tips, reached to pluck a cherry from a golden tray offered by a servant. Another stood behind her with a fan of black feathers trimmed with gold. A woman in the corner plucked gracefully on a large harp, filling the room with sweet music.

King Charles burst through the doors, not waiting for his guards to open it. Two of his men scurried in behind him as formally as they could.

"When I send for you," the king growled, "it is not a request; it is a demand."

Cora did not even look up at him, taking another cherry and biting it slowly, savoring the taste. "I was busy," her haughty, cool voice spoke without apology.

"Yes," Charles agreed sarcastically. "Clearly you have better things to do than listen to your father, your king!"

Cora sighed dramatically and sat up. "Fine, Your Majesty," she said, her voice full of mockery. "What can I do for you today?"

"Don't pretend to not know," he growled. "Rumors of your scandalous behavior continue to spread like wildfire. They say you will let any man into your bed. How am I to marry you off when your innocence cannot be proven?"

"People talk, Father," Cora said, batting her eyes with more flirt than innocence. "No man has ever entered my bed. The idea is ridiculous." She lifted her hand and began to admire her red-tipped fingers.

"You will make them believe it is true," Charles said. "I have arranged a husband for you, Prince Alabe of Westmore. He travels here in a week."

"I don't want to marry him," Cora said defiantly, pulling legs back onto her couch and leaning over the side. "I bet he is boring."

"I pray to God he is," Charles told her, "and stubborner than you."

Cora glared at her father, but he didn't pay any attention.

"If you want to be queen, you will have a king," Charles said. "Whether I like it or not, you are the heir to my throne, so start acting like it."

With that, King Charles marched out of the room in a huff and was gone.

"Titus, make sure he does not return," Cora ordered. "And bring the duke back."

Moments later a tall and handsome man walked into the room, hair ruffled and shirt barely tucked in. "I'm sorry I had to kick you out," she said with a pout. "He won't be back for another few days."

Cora wrapped her arms around the Duke and kissed him, immediately banishing her father's words.

Cora was a child when her mother died. To the king's dismay, Cora had not been a son, and her mother did not bear any more children. He was left with Cora. His disappointment that she was not a boy was made clear to her through his distance and his disapproval of everything she did. She had spent her childhood trying to be man enough, taking fighting lessons and learning sport. It only made him angrier. "A lady should act like one," he had told her. So she settled in to being the princess, and with that, a secret seductress. The bodies of dukes and officers became her new sport. It gave her power through blackmail and secrets whispered to her between the sheets. She used these to get her way in everything.

It didn't take long before rumors spread about the princess's scandalous ways, and while she paid them no mind, the king had been horrified. Cora surrounded herself with jewels, clothes, pretty things, and any man she wanted. Well, almost any man.

~

The following day, Matthew was walking with Christine through the city. She was amazed at the hustle and bustle of it all. Men flirting with her to buy colorful silks, markets full of fresh food, hunters trading their catch.

"This place is incredible," Christine said.

Matthew laughed, "You have never strolled a market before? You must be the daughter of a duke, or an heiress perhaps."

"No," she said. "I've come from a simpler life, I think. A proper one full of rules and orders. Out here amongst the madness, I feel alive and it's foreign. I love it though."

"Like it's what you've been searching for?" Matthew asked, looking down at her. She was dressed in a simple pink gown, a wide hat tied around her head with a ribbon, her long pale hair a mess in the wind. Her hand was tucked under Matthew's arm as she followed wherever he led. When he looked down at her, she blushed.

"No," she said. "But I think I'm getting closer."

Matthew's smile went wide. "Come, let me show you something."

He led her to a small tent where a man sat at a stool in front of a canvas, painting yellow tips on the oil leaves of a tree. Behind him at least twenty canvases were displayed, each more magnificent than the next. Landscapes and portraits, a pair of ladies' shoes wrapped in ribbon. Christine was drawn to them, eyes skimming over the careful strokes. The colors were glorious, the composition stunning. She could not stop looking at them.

"Matthew!" the man painting called happily, pulling Christine out of her trance. "Good to see you, my boy." He reached out his hand and shook Matthew's firmly. "And who is this gorgeous gal you've got with you?"

"Antonio, this is Christine," Matthew introduced. "Christine, meet Antonio."

"It is a pleasure," Christine gave a small curtsy.

"Oh no," Antonio said, taking her hand and pulling it to his lips. "The pleasure is all mine, sweet lady." He gave her hand a kiss and let it go.

"Your paintings are beautiful," Christine told him.

"Very kind of you," Antonia said, his feet nearly skipping. "Painting was my passion since I was a boy, to my father's dismay. Do you paint?"

"No sir," Christine said. "I don't think I could even paint a fruit bowl."

Antonia laughed. "It is not meant for everyone. That is why I get to charge so much." Antonio winked at Christine.

"You did all of these?"

"Most. They're not all mine though. See that one there?" he pointed to a painting in the corner. A man in formal dress stood with his elbow resting on a fireplace mantel, his eyes looking at something beyond the canvas, hand tucked into his pocket.

"It's incredible," Christine said. "The detail! The artist captured the man wonderfully."

"He'd better have; I'm the one who taught him," Antonio laughed. "Isn't that right, Matthew?"

Christine looked up at Matthew with surprise. "You painted this?"

"Like he said, Antonio is a good teacher," Matthew told her.

"You are very talented," Christine said.

"And you are far too kind," Matthew told her.

"What are you and this beautiful lady doing today?" Antonio asked with a twinkle in his eye.

"I am showing her around," Matthew told him. "This is Christine's first visit to Reigland."

"Is it now?" Antonio questioned. "Well, we are thrilled to have such a fine lady bless our borders."

"Thank you, sir," Christine blushed.

"You two get on then," Antonio told them. "Don't let an old man like me keep you. But, Matthew, if you know what's good for you, she'll be your next painting."

Now Christine's blush was turning crimson, her stomach a swarm of fluttering butterflies. The thought of Matthew painting her was thrilling and frightening all at once. To have his eyes study every feature. Yes, she liked the idea.

"We are leaving now before you scare Christine into the next realm," Matthew said, leading Christine further up the road.

"Be sure to bring that painting by when you're through," Antonio called after them. He laughed at himself and sat before his canvas again, his concentration absolute.

"Would you like to go for a ride?" Matthew asked.

"That sounds wonderful," Christine replied with a new skip in her step.

They walked up to the barn where the stableman was walking out with Knight following behind.

"Knight!" Christine called, letting go of Matthew and running to her horse. She wrapped her arms around his neck. He curled his big head around her and whinnied. "Oh, I'm so happy to see you, boy."

Releasing him, she looked at his long face, rubbing a hand down his soft neck. He looked healthy and well rested, and he had been cleaned as well. Noticing he was already saddled, she mounted him without hesitation, patting the side of his neck. Matthew flung himself up behind her. "May I join you?" he asked.

"Looks like you already have," she said, and before he could respond whipped the reins, jolting them swiftly forward. Matthew put his hands on her waist for balance, and Christine's hat fell to her back in the wind.

She didn't let up, riding careless and free out of the city gates and across the open country. She didn't stop until they reached the top of a hill and saw the sun dipping to hide behind the mountains. Hues of purple and pink spread across the sky. Christine was captured by the beauty and had almost forgotten the large man pressed behind her when he snugged his hands tighter around her waist. She settled back against him, her head to his chest. They sat in silence, eyes fixed on the spectacle before them, thinking more than either of them would admit aloud.

Chapter Twelve

The Queen's Prince Charming

Six Months Later

The following months had passed like a dream. Matthew spent every spare moment with Christine. They went on long walks, had picnics under a golden sun, and Christine even let Matthew paint her. It had been thrilling.

Christine continued to stay in the home of Henry and Isabell, who had become close friends. She would help them with patients, running small errands and keeping rooms clean. Henry taught her to cook, something she was very bad at, but they had fun trying.

Christine's memory had partially returned in pictures. She remembered dancing at a beautiful ball with a prince as a young girl. She remembered perching herself on a tree with a boy she believed to be a brother. And something in her memory told her that her parents were dead. She wondered if she had left her home following their passing.

After six months of living in Reigland, Christine was attending a ball. It was the first one she had been to since she was ten, and it was anticipated to be spectacular.

The king threw many balls, often at the demand of his daughter who was never satisfied. Not many minded though; it was another chance to dress up, feast, and for the men to dance with the beautiful ladies.

When night had settled over the kingdom, giving way to diamond stars that glistened brightly in the dark blue sky, a carriage pulled up in front of Henry and Isabell's home. When it came to a stop, Matthew stepped out. He was dressed in his finest uniform, his careless locks pulled behind his head. He was nervous, though he would not let it show.

Tonight, Matthew had asked to escort Christine. Of course, she accepted. He stood beside the carriage, watching the door open in keen anticipation. Henry came out with Isabell in his arm; both laughing at each other.

"Matthew, my boy!" Henry called when they were out the door. "Thank you for letting us accompany you."

"Always a pleasure," Matthew smiled at them, shaking his head.

"She will be down in just a moment," Isabell said softly to Matthew as they walked past.

Matthew went to walk up the steps when he was halted in his tracks by the stunning woman standing on the porch. His heart stopped for a moment and then raced as Christine smiled down at him. She wore a red dress, pulled tight around her waist and falling off her shoulders. The skirt fell to the floor behind her but was pulled up a little in the front by a sparkling silver pendant, revealing black satin slippers. Her white-blonde hair was pulled up in a heap, held by silver pins that sparkled and left a few tresses dangling around her face and shoulders. She was a vision.

"Good evening, Captain," Christine said, dropping in a graceful curtsy.

"My lady," he said with a bow.

Both of their hearts raced. Their eyes locked together as she descended the stairs to take his outstretched hand.

"You are a vision," he said when she rested her hand inside his. Looking down into her crystal eyes, he wanted to kiss her there. He had other plans and held back, lifting her hand and kissing her warm, soft skin. She smelled of flowers and spice.

"Thank you," Christine replied, staring into his longing eyes.

"Come on, you two, the party is at the castle," Henry said teasingly.

Christine took a deep breath, and Matthew escorted her to the carriage.

When they reached the castle, it was crowded with carriages, footmen, and ladies in the most beautiful gowns. As Matthew helped Christine out of the conveyance, she remembered the last time she went to a ball. How wonderful it had been—until it wasn't. She tensed at the thought.

"Are you alright?" Matthew asked, noting her discomfort.

"Yes," she assured him with a smile, "just a little overwhelmed. I don't think I've been to a ball in years."

"The princess spares no expense," Matthew told her. "Reigland balls are talked about for months—until the next."

"You will have a wonderful time," Isabell assured her, reaching a gloved hand to squeeze Christine's. Isabell had worn a gown of blue silk, white pearls draped around her neck. She looked beautiful, and Henry couldn't seem to let go of her.

The four of them walked into the great ballroom. Christine was entranced. It was massive, light playing across the ceiling from the many-faceted crystal drops of four chandeliers. The room was crowded with guests who created a roar of chatter. Music played, and a few couples danced. Most people were indulging themselves with food and wine. Princess Cora sat reclined on a red velvet sofa, her body draped in a tight black dress, diamonds falling from her wrists and neck, rings adorning every finger. Her black hair was around her shoulders and a golden crown sat atop her head. A small man, shorter than she, with a baby face and dressed in a prince's formal wear, stood behind her looking very uncomfortable. She was accepting one small cake after another from a servant, trying a single bite and then returning it to the tray, shooing the servant away with the flick of her wrist. She licked her fingers slowly, sucking the sugar onto her tongue and scanning the room until her eyes fell on Matthew.

Cora stood and whispered into the ear of her partner, "I will return shortly, My Prince," she said, causing a red flush to spread over the man's face. Then she stepped down into the crowd, stealing a glass of wine from a passing tray.

Matthew, Henry, Isabell, and Christine were all taking in the room when Matthew said, "the servers seem to be ignoring this part of the room. I will find us all some wine."

"That sounds wonderful," Isabell agreed. "We'll keep an eye on this beautiful lady until you get back."

Christine smiled at Matthew shyly, a bit overwhelmed by the crowd of strangers.

"I shall return in a moment," Matthew promised with a squeeze of Christine's hand. It caused a wonderful shudder to run through her body. Then he was gone.

"It's clearly working," Isabell said slyly when Matthew was out of sight. "He can barely keep his eyes off of you."

Christine bit her lip. "He looks so handsome in his uniform," she said.

"Ah yes, ladies and your men in uniforms," Henry said.

Isabell elbowed him in the ribs. "I dare say he is more interested in that dress you're wearing," Isabell said, "or how you look in it, anyway."

"Do you think?" Christine questioned.

Henry laughed aloud. "No thinking about it. You have that man wrapped around your dainty finger."

"I wager he makes a move tonight," Isabell said.

"Anyone who would wager against you would be a fool," Henry agreed.

Matthew was sliding through the crowd in search of drink, pressed against the far wall by the mass of bodies. Long, slender fingers grabbed his arm and pulled him behind one of the black drapes. He found himself against the wall, Cora pressing her whole body against him. "There you are, Captain," she whispered in his ear. "I've been waiting all night for you to join me."

"Please, Princess," Matthew said, pushing her arms, trying to escape her demand. "I won't be one of your playthings."

"Playthings?" Cora asked in fake astonishment. "Whatever are you talking about?" She pressed harder to him, fighting against his efforts for escape.

"The king would have my head," he whispered.

"You know that old bastard would give me anything I wanted," Cora argued. "Come on, you know you want to make my body yours again."

"And I have fallen for someone else," Matthew told her.

Cora laughed a loud and mocking laugh. "Oh come on, you really expect me to believe you want some floozy more than the future Queen of Reigland?"

"That is exactly what I am saying," Matthew told her. "We will never happen."

He turned and pushed her against the wall, gaining the advantage.

"Oh, come on," she pleaded. "It's not like you have never done it before."

"That was a long time ago," Matthew said. "It will never happen again."

She swiftly moved her arms between his, sliding his hands aside, and wrapped her arms around him. She combed cold fingers behind his neck, causing him to shudder, and whispered in his ear, "But don't you remember how good it felt? Our bodies tangled together. So what if my father despises it; that's what makes it so exciting."

She trailed her hand down his chest and he caught her wrist, pulling her away. "No," he said strongly. "I am not yours anymore."

He escaped her grasp and moved away from her. She called after him, "I'm Princess Cora, Captain. I always get what I want. Eventually."

She leaned against the wall and watched him walk away, then caught the eye of the prince who stood waiting for her, his face sour. She walked over to him and ran her cold hand down the side of his face. "Do you like what you see?" she asked.

"You do not act as a princess should," he scolded. "If you wish to be my wife, you'll behave as a wife does."

"Or what?" she asked. "You mean to threaten me when you are the one with a chance to be king? And trust me," she said, her hand trailing down his chest and stomach before whispering in his ear, "I'll make it all worth it."

When Matthew found a server with a tray full of wine, he threw back a glass before taking more for the others.

"It took you long enough," Isabell scolded when he returned. "Where did you get off to?"

"It is a ball, not the easiest room to navigate," Matthew defended, handing them each a glass.

"Thank you," Christine said and took a sip of wine.

A loud clang drew everyone's attention to the king who now stood before them.

"It is a good day in Reigland," he said. "Change is upon us, I hope for the better. A new day and with it, a new generation. I am pleased to announce the official engagement of my daughter Princess Cora to Prince Alabe of Westmore."

The crowd erupted in cheers. Cora took Alabe's hand and raised it up, her public smile plastered so well on her face, any would think her sincere.

"That's so exciting," Christine said, clapping her hands with joy. "A prince to marry a princess; it's just so wonderful."

"I feel sorry for the poor gent," Henry said. "How long do you think he will last?"

"Three months," Isabell said.

"No," Matthew disagreed. "The king is not well. She knows if she doesn't tie herself to a husband, she forfeits the throne. Cora won't give up the throne, not for anything."

"She doesn't love him?" Christine asked in astonishment.

Isabell laughed. "Oh you sweet girl, I will tell you about Cora and her scandals later. We could talk all night long about it."

"Yes," Henry said. "And right now, I just want a dance with my wife." Henry bowed, extending his hand to Isabell. "My lady, may I have this dance?"

Isabell gave a giggle and curtsy. "It would be my pleasure, sir."

Taking his hand, Isabell followed Henry to the dance floor where they wrapped arms around each other and began to sway. He whispered things into her ear, and Isabell laughed and shook her head at him.

"They are the sweetest couple," Christine said, staring at them dance.

"Henry and Isabell are a match born in the heavens," Matthew agreed. He then bowed to Christine and extended his hand. "Would you give me the honor of a dance?"

Christine was terrified, she had a bad feeling in her gut from the last time she danced with a man. The Prince's gentle smile followed by an overwhelming horror. But this was a different place, and she was older now. Lord knew her body ached to dance, especially with the handsome captain.

"The honor would be mine," Christine agreed with a curtsy and accepted his offered hand.

Christine was taking deep breaths in and out, heart beating fast as they walked onto the floor. *Just breathe, control it, follow his lead.* He turned to face her, wrapped his hand around her waist, combing fingers through her other hand. She put her hand on his shoulder and let him pull her close. Beginning with a single step, their bodies moved in graceful sync. Every step matched, every turn held close. Her body surrendered to his lead, and they turned around the dance floor, eyes locked, hearts pounding against each other.

Cora noticed the two of them dancing and she fumed, eyes glaring at Matthew as he spun Christine around.

"Would you like to dance?" Alabe asked her.

"No," she said simply through gritted teeth.

Matthew and Christine were lost in each other as if they were the only people on earth. It was just the two of them, hand in hand, step by step, dancing through the stars. It was glorious, wonderful and only the beginning.

When the music came to an end, Christine began to pull away, but Matthew coaxed her back in. "Wait here, don't move," he instructed. He walked over and whispered something to the conductor.

Then he returned to Christine with a broad smile and took her back in his arms. The floor was clearing when the violin struck; immediately they were off. Christine felt something deep inside awaken, rise and take over. Within seconds, she was soaring, free as a bird through the morning sky. Or that's how it seemed, anyway. Nothing to hold her back, she danced with everything she had. In this moment Christine knew, she found what she had been looking for. She found herself.

At the last note, Christine wrapped her leg around Matthew's and bent her back, head flung out with undone hair. As he pulled her back up, she found herself face to face with Matthew. He drew her to him and kissed her hard. No one in the world but the two of them.

Moving apart, they just stared at each other, catching their breath. The white noise settled, and they realize everyone around them was screaming and cheering.

"Brava!"

"Amazing!"

"Incredible!"

"Encore!"

Christine threw her head back in laughter, feeling life swell through her entire body.

"Come," Matthew said, taking her hand and pulling her through the adoring crowd. They slid through the back and out a door, finding themselves on the terrace. When they were away from the crowd, beneath the night sky, Matthew stopped and looked down at Christine.

"What is it?" she asked him.

"Christine," he said, "I do not think it is a secret that the day you showed up in Reigland, I was enchanted, captivated by you."

Christine's heart beat fast. The look in his eyes almost dangerous.

"I became certain very quickly that I wanted to know you. And as I knew you, I never wanted to spend a moment without you. I want to be there, with you, for every moment of the rest of your life."

Her hand in his, Matthew moved down to his knee before her.

"Matthew—" Christine breathed out.

"I want to ask you something," Matthew said. Then he pulled a sparkling diamond out of his pocket. Christine threw her hand over her mouth, tears prickling at her eyes.

"If you let me, I will spend the rest of my life giving you everything I am," he said, looking up at her with pleading eyes. "I love you, Christine; you hold my heart, my destiny. Will you be my wife, allow me to be your husband, and grow old side by side?"

Slowly she began to nod her head as he slipped the ring on her finger and stood, staring deep into her eyes. "Is that a yes?"

"Yes," she said. And he claimed her mouth with his, lifting her feet off the ground. He spun in joyful circles, her feet kicked up behind her.

~

"Champagne!" Henry lifted a bottle in the air, popping the cork. Bubbles fell over his hand as he poured glasses.

"More?" Isabell asked, leaning over his arm.

"We are celebrating," he said, lifting two glasses and carrying them to the sitting room where Matthew and Christine sat like smitten children on a playground bench. "For these two lovebugs. You dog, Matthew, why didn't you say anything about proposing tonight?"

"Because you would have spoiled it," Matthew stated, raising his glass in thanks.

"He's right," Isabell sang, handing a glass to Henry.

"I would not have," Henry defended in astonishment, looking from Isabell to Matthew to Christine. They all laughed at him. "Okay, maybe I would have."

"Well, what matters is we all know now," Christine said, raising her glass to clink it with the others.

"Here, here," Isabell agreed. Right before she took a sip of her Champagne, she added under her breath, "I knew."

Henry spit his drink back into his glass. "You knew?"

Isabell shrugged innocently. "You would have spilled. Like you just did." She took a napkin and dabbed his chin. He leaned in and kissed her, shutting off the conversation.

"Well I am happy to celebrate with all of you," Matthew said, his hand clasped to Christine's. "In the peace and quiet."

"Oh yes, speaking of," Isabell said as she took the seat adjacent to Matthew and Christine. "Did you see the look Princess Cora was giving you during your show-stopping dance?"

"The princess?" Christine asked. "Why?"

"Oh, she has been in love with Matthew here for years now," Henry told her. "Obsessed with him actually."

"With Matthew?" Christine laughed more than she meant.

"Not that I care, but is it so hard to believe?" Matthew asked.

"Of course not," Christine assured him with a squeeze of the hand. "I am just saying, it shocks me that a woman who will marry a prince would home in on the captain of her father's guard."

"There is no soul on earth who can explain the Princess of Reigland," Henry said. "She does what she wants, how she wants, and no one can stop her. Her father should have been sterner with her in childhood."

"Or been there at all," Isabell said. "As awful as she can be, inside she is just a little girl who wants her father to notice her."

"My first ball in years and I end up on the bad side of a royal," Christine said uncomfortably.

"Being on the bad side of Princess Cora just means you showed up," Henry assured her.

"Well she's engaged now," Isabell said. "Perhaps having a man by her side will help."

"We'll keep dreaming anyway," Matthew said into his drink.

"Matthew is right," Henry agreed. "I don't think any law or ring will ever stop Cora from being Cora."

"Well, you are engaged now too," Christine said dreamily, leaning into Matthew.

"That I am," Matthew said before kissing her. "And hope to be a married man before the year ends."

"Here, here," Henry toasted in agreement.

Chapter Thirteen

Seduced By A Princess

"He's marrying her?" Princess Cora screamed in fury, flinging her glass against the wall. Crystal shattered; blood-red wine ran down the wall.

The spy who was reporting to Cora was shaking with fear. "He asked her the night of the ball. She said yes."

"Well, of course, she said yes," Cora said in annoyance and began to pace. "Bloody lunatic!"

"Your Majesty," the man pressed cautiously, "as future queen, surely you can have any man you want. I hear you are betrothed to a prince. What is it about this man that you must have him?"

Cora walked to her window, pressing aside the sheer curtain and looking out at her kingdom. "Have you ever been in love, Theo?" she asked.

"Well, I'm not sure about love, Majesty," he said. "Fancied a bonny or two."

"No," she said, "You cannot understand." She turned back to the room and moved gracefully across the floor. "The captain and I have something special, even if he forgets. He will be mine."

"He is marrying another," Theo said, instantly wishing he hadn't as Cora pierced him with deathly eyes.

"Mere titles and promised words to another are not enough to take him from me." She settled down onto her couch, accepting a fresh glass of wine from a maid. "First I claim my throne. Then, mark my words, he will be mine."

Theo bowed in surrender.

"Continue to follow him," Cora instructed, "and inform me of any inevitable change."

"As you command, My Princess." Theo bowed low and exited the room.

"Tyla!" Cora yelled as soon as Theo had left.

A skittish woman hurried into the room in short, quick steps. "Yes, Majesty?"

"Have my horse readied. I have prey to hunt."

"As you wish, Majesty." The timid woman turned and hurried back out of the room.

Cora ran a bony finger across the rim of her glass, thinking back to the ball and that disastrous dance. How could Matthew love a common girl more than he loved her? Just like her father, more wrapped in his kingdom than his own daughter. And now betrothed to a man who could barely pass as a man himself; she was disgusted.

Rising from her seat, she let a servant wrap her in a riding cloak, her dark eyes glittering with determination from under the hood.

She rode out with two bodyguards, galloping across the plains of Reigland, hooves pounding the ground, throwing clumps of dirt in their wake. When they spotted the king's riders in the distance, Cora gave a smile so small it could only be seen in her eyes.

"Halt!" one of her guards yelled. "Prepare for the princess!"

Matthew halted his men and looked back to see Cora and her men hurrying towards them. Dismounting his horse, he stepped before his men and awaited their approach.

"Your Majesty," Matthew said when they caught up, "to what do we owe this unexpected meet?"

"News of your engagement reached me," Cora said, making an effort to sound pleasant. "My congratulations to you and Belinda."

"Christine," Matthew corrected in annoyance.

"Hm," Cora assessed him with her eyes.

"Is there something I can assist you with, Majesty?" Matthew asked, anger beginning to rise.

"As a matter of fact," Cora said, a long finger tapping her chin, "my betrothed is making his way to Reigland as we speak. I wish you to ensure that the security between his new chambers and my own is not lacking."

"I will send Troy to set a guard," Matthew offered.

"I think it best you do this yourself," Cora instructed. "This is for the prince, not some commoner."

"My concern is the protection of the whole kingdom," Matthew stated, "including all who reside within the castle walls. I trust all of these men with my life and the lives of every man in Reigland. You can trust Troy with anything you need."

Cora dismounted, removed the hood of her cloak and stepped close to Matthew.

"One day," she said so quietly that no other could hear, "you will realize the mistake you are making, and you will come back to me."

"I pray I never see the day," Matthew said. "I have bound myself to Christine, and you will not pull us apart unless you kill me."

Cora narrowed her piercing eyes at him and without a word returned to her horse.

"Send Troy then," she ordered, before turning with her men and galloping away.

"That woman could turn fire to ice with a single glare," Troy said with a shiver.

"Please check the safety of the prince we will be adopting as soon as we return," Matthew told him.

Troy nodded once, and the men were off again.

~

Troy walked down the hall on his way to see the princess when Tyla pulled him into a secret passage behind a large painting.

"What is the meaning of this?" he asked.

"Sh, please, sir," Tyla pleaded in a whisper. They were in complete darkness, but Tyla held a small candle, which gave a little light. "Her Majesty wishes your presence."

"That is why I am going to see her," Troy stated, not understanding.

"You must follow a different path," Tyla whispered.

"What path to the princess would the king's guard not know?" Troy asked.

"The one the princess's guard watches," Tyla said as though revealing a secret path to the lost ark.

Troy paused, a bad feeling in his gut. He decided it best to follow Cora's instructions.

"Lead the way, madam," he said and followed Tyla through a narrow, black hall, taking a turn here and there, his hand clasped on the head of his sword. Troy memorized his path carefully, assuring himself he could find his way out. Finally, they stepped through a door that Troy realized was behind a painting on the wall, and they were in Princess Cora's washroom.

Steam rose from a large pool in the ground. Even with the fog, Troy saw Cora in a thin robe, dipping her toe into the water. She turned her head over her shoulder to see the uncomfortable soldier entering the bathing room. She offered her most seductive smile.

"Troy, so good of you to come," she said. And just like that, she let the robe slip from her shoulders, off her body, crumpling into a pile of silk on the floor. She was now bare before him. Troy's eyes wandered involuntarily over the princess's smooth curves. She walked gracefully down the steps until the water reached the crown of her breasts. She felt his eyes lingering as she sank beneath the ripples, then rose out of the water with a long drag of air, her head thrown back, allowing the water to pull her hair slick behind her. She smoothed hands over her wet hair and perched on a seat, smiling at the man gawking.

Troy was stunned silent, swallowing hard, his heart beating fast. He wasn't sure if he had just entered the door to heaven or hell. All he knew for sure was that he didn't want to leave. A small noise drew his attention. He turned to see Tyla disappear through the secret passage, leaving him alone with Cora.

"As long as you come to see me through the passage," Cora told him sweetly, "no one will ever know you were here. Not even your captain." Cora lifted her fingers out of the water and idly inspected her blood-red nails.

Troy was near panting, his entire body alert. "You sent for me—security—your betrothed prince," he fumbled.

"Oh, the prince my father has arranged for me to marry?" Cora asked as if something dull had been placed in her mouth. "If he were to be assassinated, I would give whoever saved me—whatever they wanted in reward."

Cora's eyes pierced Troy with a thousand silent questions. Though he was the one standing in full armor, he felt vulnerable and a little frightened.

"What do you want from me, My Princess?" Troy asked breathlessly.

"I want you to bathe," she said, words falling from her lips like sugar. "And then we can discuss how you would feel in the princess's guard."

"I shall return then," Troy said, turning to leave.

"Wait, why are you leaving?" Cora asked.

"Clean myself as you command, Majesty," Troy said.

Cora gave him a half smile, spreading her arms over the marble side of the bathing pool. "The water in here is perfect."

Troy thought his heart would explode it beat so hard within his chest. Cora stared at him with her frightening dark eyes, daring him. He'd heard tales, rumors about the princess and her scandals. He did not want to be one of them; Matthew would destroy him. But more than that, he wanted to be in that pool.

"Don't you like what you see?" Cora asked, the slightest tilt of her head evading innocence.

"Yes," Troy breathed.

"He will never know," Cora assured him, answering the unspoken question.

Uncomfortably, Troy began to remove his armor, placing it carefully to the side. He thought he might be about to die but thought this would be the ideal way to go out. As he exposed himself, Cora let her eyes wander over his body. He was not as handsome as Matthew, but he was fit and would serve his purpose well enough. He followed where Cora had ascended the steps, hot water biting his flesh until he was sitting on a seat on the opposite side of the bath. Cora gave a laugh as if accepting his challenge and moved over to where he was, pressing her body against his, her legs straddling his waist. Her arms wrapped around his neck, combing fingers through his hair. Troy's body was stiff and sensitive, his breathing very shallow.

"Is it warm enough?" she asked, suddenly seeming innocent and small.

"Yes, My Princess," he replied hoarsely. "Thank you."

Troy put his hands on her hips beneath the water and lost control, his scruples disappearing as she shuddered her appreciation.

"I need you to ask me something," Cora whispered into his ear, sending tingles down his spine. "Does your alliance lie with the captain of the king's guard, with the king himself, or with your princess who wants to give you the world?"

He would have answered very differently the day before, but now he knew what he had to say. With her body so gloriously entwining with his, what he wanted to say. "My alliance lies unwavering with you, My Princess," he breathed, hands climbing her back and pulling her onto him.

"Good," she groaned. "You will do exactly what I tell you to, no matter the cost. And in return, you will be greatly rewarded—with me."

"With you?"

Grazing fingernails across his flesh, she whispered in his ear, "I will make fantasies come true that you never knew you had."

"As you command," he said, barely understanding her words but knowing he would give Cora anything she ever asked for.

~

Bells rang, music played, roses of white and women in their best clothes filled the royal terrace to a chorus of giggles and whispers. A flutter of excitement filled the streets as everyone within the Kingdom of Reigland gathered to celebrate the wedding of Princess Cora to Prince Alabe. Well, almost everyone.

Outside of Reigland, overlooking the sea, Matthew and Christine joined hands before a priest. Christine was in a gown of white; Matthew wore his handsome black captain's uniform with red trim. The only guests were Henry and Isabell, who hugged close together watching. The wind blew, trying to carry hair and dress away with it. Matthew and Christine barely noticed, hand in hand, lost in each other's eyes.

"Captain?" the priest pulled Matthew out of his lovesick trance.

"What?"

"Do you take Christine?"

"Oh," Matthew laughed at himself, staring back into Christine's eyes with deep sincerity. "I do. Until my last breath and with everything I have. I do."

"Aw," Isabell squeezed Henry tightly, wiping a happy tear from her eye.

"And do you, Christine, take Matthew?" the priest continued.

"Oh, I do," Christine answered without looking away from Matthew.

"Then by the power vested in me by God, I pronounce you man and wife."

"Yeah!" Henry yelled as he and Isabell both clapped with joy.

Matthew needed no more prompting. He dipped Christine in his arms and pressed his lips to hers. "I love you," he said.

"I love you," she replied.

"They finally did it!" Isabell squeezed Henry again. Both of them were beaming with pride and joy.

"They better get to work; I'm ready to be an uncle," Henry said.

Matthew and Christine just laughed and embraced each other.

In the back of Christine's mind, she wondered if she had a family out there. The brother she thought she remembered. Perhaps her parents were alive. Even if she couldn't remember, she somehow wished they were there with her. Maybe one day.

At the castle, the wedding of the prince and princess had taken over. Everyone wanted to get at least a glimpse of the princess in her wedding gown, lining the streets in expectation. She was a vision of beauty, but her eyes were hard and her body stiff. Her prince appeared more uncomfortable than joyous, like a fish pulled from the sea and stuffed into a small glass bowl.

After the ceremony and a celebration, which they left early, Prince Alabe and Princess Cora consummated their marriage.

As he lay breathless beneath the sheets, Alabe had a moment when he thought things had finally come together. Perhaps Reigland could be home to him, and he and his princess could be happy, having many children. But this feeling was stolen from him quickly.

"Unless I am bored one night," Cora said, "this is the last time you will have me in your bed."

Cora moved from the bed, wrapping herself in a robe. Alabe sat up, staring at her with a gaping mouth.

"Feel free to bed whoever you want," Cora said. "It makes no difference to me. I'll be doing the same."

"You can't do this," Alabe said. "I am your husband, your prince; you are to obey me." He rose from the bed, hurrying to stop her. He grabbed her arm. "Come back here!"

She pulled a small knife—he could not even tell from where—and put it to his throat. He was in shock; no one had ever threatened him before. He was a prince of Westmore! But her eyes were dangerous, and he knew she would not hesitate to kill him.

"You are my husband so that I can be queen," she said as if he were slow-witted. "Get in my way, and you will not live to see another sunrise."

He let go of her arm and she turned to leave again.

"I'll go to your father," Alabe sputtered. "Surely he will not approve."

Cora threw her head back in laughter. "Go to my father," she dared. "Our marriage has been consummated, and as the younger of five brothers, the only way you will ever wear the crown of a king is if you are by my side. I am giving you every man's dream. You can bed any woman in Reigland, and I won't blink an eye. Have the maids, have the ladies. Just make sure no bastards bother me. You will wear the crown of the king; your every wish will be granted. All you have to do is shut up and remain in your place. To the public, we will be a devoted couple. I am no fool; I know the kingdom needs what appears to be a real marriage to ease their minds. But within these walls, this is as far as we go."

"But what about—an heir?" he said.

"Oh, I don't know. I'll likely call one of your bastards my own and let that be the end of it."

Cora left the room, and Alabe hung his head, rubbing frustrated hands through his hair. His wedding night gone from glorious to disastrous, and there was nothing he could do about it.

Cora returned to her chambers to find Troy beneath her sheets, waiting for her. "Come to bed, My Princess," he invited, pulling down the covers beside him.

Cora let her hair down over her shoulders, shaking it out, black ripples falling around her. Removing her robe, she slid in beside Troy and kissed him deeply.

"Is it done?" Troy asked her.

"Yes, my love," she cooed, running her cold fingers down his torso. "The prince will be of no more bother to us. And neither will my father."

Growling his approval, Troy moved over and claimed his princess.

Chapter Fourteen

Death of a King

Christine lay on the bed, her head at the foot and her feet resting on Matthew's bare chest. She was lost in a book, a fairytale of faraway lands. Matthew brushed his thumb over the birthmark on her ankle. He had always thought it was beautiful, something special and unique to her.

As if off in another world, Matthew began speaking, "When I was a boy, there were legends told of a place full of magic."

Christine laid her book on her stomach, turning her attention to Matthew. "What kind of magic?"

"They said the royals were all magic. The men and women alike were born with the ability to dance better than the best dancers in the world. They learned dancing as a child learns to walk, at least it was said. Their dances were exquisite, beyond anything anyone had ever seen, captivating a room. And you could always tell they were of royal blood because of the distinct rose on their ankles."

"A rose?" Christine asked, "you must be playing with me."

"It's what the legend said," Matthew insisted. "Conveniently though, the kingdom was destroyed."

"Never existed, more like," Christine said. "What a wonderful tale, though. I imagine a place like that would always be full of happiness."

Matthew moved from beneath her legs and turned to lie beside her, weight resting on his elbows. She looked up into his eyes. "No place could be as happy as when I am beside you. Especially when you carry our baby." He placed his hand on her slightly rounded stomach, just far enough along to show.

She pressed her hand to the side of his face, her crystal eyes looking deep into his. "If this is what heaven feels like, I'd wish to die today, but only if it meant you by my side for eternity."

He bent his head and kissed her lovingly, her body turning to him in response. "I love you," he said.

"And I you, my sweet captain."

Matthew and Christine were startled by the sound of a rider racing down the street calling loudly. Matthew rose to his feet and looked out the window.

"The king is dead!" the rider called.

"The king is dead?" Christine asked in disbelief, hearing the cry.

Matthew went to his chest for a shirt and began to dress. "They'll be knocking on the door any moment. My presence will be required at the castle."

Christine pulled her knees to her chest, resting her chin on them like a frightened child in the night. "Poor king. What does this mean for us—for Reigland?"

"It means Prince Alabe and Princess Cora will be crowned king and queen. And with that, I will be named the captain of their guard. And a new king and queen means an adjustment for the whole kingdom. There will be pushback. The dear princess is not trusted; many refuse to serve her."

"She won't do anything awful, will she?" Christine asked.

Matthew moved over to the bed and sat next to her. "It's been five months since her wedding, and she hasn't caused any problems. I hope it is a sign that everything will remain calm."

Christine looked at him with big round eyes and a small pout. She didn't want him to leave, but she knew he was needed and didn't say anything.

"Oh, my love," he said, brushing the hair from her face. "I promise you, this will not change anything for us. My duty is to the kingdom; my heart belongs to you and our child."

She smiled at him, and he gave her a kiss. Then three loud bangs came from the front door.

"I won't let anything happen to us," Matthew assured her. "I promise, I shall return as soon as I can."

"I will be waiting."

Matthew rode to the castle where his men had already set extra units around the outside of the walls. With the news of the king's death, crowds had drawn in swarms, demanding to know more. Matthew made his way to the throne room where Alabe and Cora spoke with their advisors.

"We must bury your father," one of the men in rich clothes and golden pendants was telling Cora. "And tomorrow crown you both King and Queen of Reigland. The people must have time to grieve, but they will also want to know this does not affect their lives or safety. They need to see a firm leader in place."

"When can we be ready to escort my father's body?" Cora asked.

"It can be done late this afternoon," the man told her.

"We should give them a day," Matthew said, joining their small group. "I understand we need to send the king off with the greatest respect, but the crowds are bewildered. Give it a day to settle and news to finish spreading. We can do it tomorrow."

"Fine," Cora said. "Then I want to be crowned."

"Your Majesty, a ball must be set—" the man tried to object.

"Then do it," Cora demanded. "My husband and I will be ready. I want to be crowned by tonight."

She turned and marched off before anyone could object, leaving behind a frenzy of servants and leaders trying to bring order back to the throne room.

"Your Majesty," Matthew called, following behind Cora and Alabe.

Cora turned to him when they had reached the hall. "My dear Captain, have you come to bed me now that I am queen?"

"Your Majesty, you have a husband. A husband who is right beside you. Have you no shame?" Matthew asked.

"My King and I have an understanding," she said into Alabe's ear, running her finger down the side of his cheek to his throat. Alabe's blood ran cold. "As for you, your wife must not be as appealing with a babe on the way."

Michael was enraged but contained himself as best he could. "Do not speak of my wife or our child. I am the Captain of your Guard now and should be respected as such."

Cora laughed, "I always did love that sense of humor you have. Now if you'll excuse me, my husband and I must get ready for our ceremony."

Cora took Alabe's hand to lead him away, but Matthew stopped him.

"Your Majesty, it is not a good idea to throw all of this on the people at once. It will be chaos."

"And that is your concern," Cora said flatly. "Mine is to give the people what they want: a queen. Do your job, and I will do mine."

Cora turned, and she and Alabe disappeared down the hall. Matthew spent the day setting extra stations all through the castle, he and his men fighting off the mobs. Reinforcements were sent into the kingdom as well, the chaos spreading to the boarder.

The night brought a new king and queen to Reigland, and the people were not happy. Cora was called the Devil Queen, her reputation preceding her. Many did not want to live under her reign. It took months for the riots to stop and the towns to return to normal. Matthew was away more than usual, the chaos demanding every free moment.

Christine spent most of her time with Henry and Isabell. Henry worried over Christine; every time she moved suddenly, he hurried to see if she was alright. Isabell thought by the way Christine carried she would be having a girl.

"She's never been wrong," Henry told Christine.

"A girl," Christine thought, rubbing her round belly. "How wonderful."

Cora was proving to be a trial, far more wrapped up in her balls and riches than in her people. Her husband the king provided no help, acting like a mute and barely leaving his chambers. Rumors circled that the king and queen never visited each other, but that each took lovers of their own, their marriage merely for political gain. This increased the disapproval of the people.

Time passed. Christine's belly grew, and Matthew stole every moment he could to be with his wife, even if the moments were fleeting. Returning home to slide in next to her sleeping body, he would often be gone by the time she woke. They cherished every moment, and Matthew continued promising that things would get better soon. One day their lives would return to the steady hours and peaceful domesticity they loved.

Christine believed him and loved him more for it. Though she was lonely, she rested in the hope things would be right again soon.

~

Cora was lounging on a sofa in the throne room, which was made of gold. She was dripping in jewels and clad in seductive clothing. Alabe sat near her, spending far too long inspecting a cake that had been handed to him. Advisors and dukes were discussing the dissatisfaction of the people, but Cora was paying them no mind.

A guard entered and announced loudly, "Your Majesties, a man from Hanton wishes to speak to you."

Cora turned her gaze to Alabe, who flicked his hand. "Send him in."

A man entered in rider's clothing, dirty with dust and looking very tired. When he was before them, Alabe said, "What is your name, sir?"

"Sir David of Hanton." He bowed before the king and queen.

"And what business do you have in Reigland?" Alabe asked.

"I am searching for a girl," David began.

"Aren't we all?" A man yelled from the back, his comment followed by laughter through the room.

Ignoring him, David continued, "She would be about twenty now. Raised in Hanton under the care of myself and my wife. She ran away when she turned eighteen. I have been looking for her since. Your Majesty, she does not know, but she is the rightful queen to a throne, the last of royal blood. It is very important that I find her. She is about average height, hair almost white and eyes so blue they look like crystal."

Cora's eyes rose from the wine she had been studying idly. Her heart was beginning to beat rapidly. She knew that description; she knew it all too well.

"The way you would be sure it is her, she would have a mark on her ankle that looks like a rose. Her name is Christine," he finished.

Alabe opened his mouth, but Cora quickly rose and put a hand on his leg, stopping him from speaking. Her mind flashed back to the night of her ball, how Christine had danced with Matthew, and that mark on her ankle, which had puzzled Cora. It suddenly all made sense and yet didn't.

"How could a queen be lost from her own kingdom?" Cora asked. "Surely it is not possible. Are you a madman or just remarkably irresponsible?"

"No, Your Majesty," David insisted. "I assure you. Queen Christine was the only remaining heir to the throne of Dancé."

"Dancé is merely a legend our fathers told us," Alabe dismissed.

"Destroyed years ago, it is true," David admitted. "Christine was but a baby, so we hid her away, thinking we were protecting her. She has been gone for two years now, and I am desperate. We have rebuilt Dancé. Even now a few live in its walls, under the leadership of the King of Hanton. We want our queen to return home."

"Perhaps your queen does not want to be found," Cora said, "or is dead."

"Not dead," David said. "I know in my heart she is alive. She lost the woman she knew as her mother, and she ran. She does not know her birthright; I am sure she simply found comfort in a land far from home. I just want to know she is safe."

"I understand your desperation, Sir David, but we are not hosting a girl matching your description," Cora told him. "My guards keep me apprised of strangers who settle here." She noticed a couple of the guards exchanging glances and demanded with her eyes that everyone be silent. "We do have many pass through our borders. She could have traveled straight through, and I wouldn't have been told. I will be glad to make inquiries for you. I am sorry to say though; she is not here. Please, you must be exhausted from your journey. We will ready a room and you can rest before returning to the road."

"That is very kind, Your Majesty," David said. "I must continue on. Please, if you see her, anyone, tell her that we miss her and want her home. And if you'd be so kind as to send word following your inquiries. Any news or clue would make me forever grateful."

"I will have men on the lookout and send word if we see her," Cora said, sounding frighteningly sincere. Alabe glanced at her, confused, but wisely kept his mouth shut.

"I thank you." David bowed, turned and left.

"He means the wife of the captain," Alabe whispered loudly to Cora when David was gone. "Why did you not tell him?"

"Oh, my dear husband," Cora said, smoothing a hand over Alabe's check. He never liked when she touched him tenderly; he knew it was a threat. "And have the wife of the man I love be given a crown? Remain silent. This David man will never find her. No one will."

"I thought you had moved on from the captain," Alabe argued. "Taken that Troy fellow."

Cora narrowed her eyes.

"What?" He put up his hands defensively. "We may not share a bed, but it's not hard to know who you spend your hours with."

"Stay out of my business, husband," Cora hissed, "unless you want to wake with a knife in your throat."

Cora rose and left the room in a fury. Having seen and heard everything that had happened, Troy followed her back to the chambers. When they were safely inside, Troy put his arms around Cora. "What is bothering you?"

"That wench. A queen? Does she want my crown as well as my heart? Damn her. Damn her!" She turned and buried herself into Troy's chest.

"Sh," Troy soothed, smoothing the silk-straight hair on her head. "He is gone now."

"But he will come back," Cora said angrily, pulling away and walking to stare out the window. "We are lucky Matthew wasn't here; he would have betrayed us."

"What do you want me to do?" Troy asked.

Cora stared silently at the terrace below, a carriage riding past, servants trimming the well-manicured bushes. The sun was close to setting, shining orange rays straight through her window.

"Bring him to me," Cora ordered.

Without a word, Troy left the room, understanding it was not his place to ask questions.

Matthew was mounting his horse to return home to Christine. He missed her terribly and was ready to see her, especially since the baby was due any day. Before he could leave, though, Troy came running to him.

"Captain!" Troy called.

Matthew turned his horse to face Troy. "Is it urgent? I want to go home to my wife."

"I am sorry, Captain," Troy said, "but Her Majesty requires your immediate presence."

"Tell her I will see her tomorrow."

Matthew pulled the reins to turn, but Troy caught the end. "The queen insists."

Matthew stared at Troy in confusion. He was never one to argue with Matthew when he said he was doing something. It must be especially urgent for Troy to persist, but Matthew wanted to be home badly.

"Can it not wait?" Matthew tried once more.

"I am sorry," Troy repeated. "She insists."

With a heavy sigh, Matthew dismounted his horse, allowing a nearby horseman to take the reins. "This better be a matter of life and death."

Matthew followed Troy back into the castle. They wound through halls, their boots echoing off the walls, walking up stairs. Matthew sensed something was wrong; he had never seen Troy like this, insisting that he come, even if it was by Cora's command.

"What is really going on?" Matthew asked.

"The queen demanded to see you," Troy said, not turning to look at Matthew.

"Yes, you said that," Matthew said. "Why?"

"I do not know," Troy insisted. "I am the escort, not the messenger."

"I need an escort, do I?" Matthew asked.

"No," Troy stammered. "Well, yes. No—she just wanted me to bring you to her. That is what she commanded; I am simply obeying. Damn it, man, just move."

Troy led Matthew to one of the castle sitting rooms. Opening the door, he gestured for Matthew to enter.

"Why in here?" Matthew asked, his feet planted on the ground.

"Queen's orders," Troy said simply.

"Her Majesty seems to be giving a lot of orders that don't make sense lately," Matthew mumbled, moving past Troy and entering the small sitting room.

As soon as he was inside the door, Troy pressed it closed. Matthew's ear perked at the sound of a lock. Turning quickly, he tried the door, but it wouldn't give. He banged a strong fist on the hard wood. "Damn you, Troy! Open the door!"

Silence. He was trapped, alone, left with nothing but questions.

Chapter Fifteen

City of Blood and Fire

"Breathe, breathe," Isabell said calmly to Christine who was in anguishing labor. "That's it, now push. Hard as you can, push."

Christine held her breath and pushed with all of her might, grunting loudly, teeth clenched, willing herself not to scream. They'd been at it for hours, Henry and Isabell spending all day at the home of Matthew and Christine, working with her. The baby was ready, but the labor was hard.

Sweat poured out all over Christine's body. Henry assisting, Isabell patiently worked with Christine to help her. Unable to push anymore, Christine threw her head back and sucked in heavy breaths. "I can't do it anymore."

Henry took her hand. "You can; you must."

Christine shook her head. "Where is Matthew? I need him here."

"I sent word," Henry assured her. "He will be here."

"It's time to push again," Isabell said. "The baby is right here. You can do it, Christine. Push."

Henry helped her lean back up, sucking a breath she pushed with everything she had. Calling out, she felt as if her insides were tearing apart. Henry gritted his teeth, believing his hand was possibly broken from how hard she squeezed, but he didn't pull away. And then there was a cry, a small cry, somehow quiet and very loud all at once.

"It's a girl," Isabell said, taking the purple-skinned, screaming baby and laying her on Christine's chest before returning to her task of caring for Christine.

"Oh my God," Christine cried, looking at the tiny person in her arm in utter amazement. "She is the most beautiful thing I have ever seen."

"Dirty little bug," Henry joked. "Needs a bath."

Christine laughed a little through her cries, the small baby grabbing her finger. Looking down on the fragile ankle of her baby, she saw the rose, which marked her. The baby bore the same mark, and her head was covered in downy white hair with only a hint of yellow. "She is perfect."

"Does the little lady have a name?" Henry asked.

"Alexandra," Christine said quietly, never moving her eyes from the small baby who settled against her chest. "I never knew love could be this strong so quickly. I think my heart might leap from my chest. I don't ever want to let her go."

Isabell came around to look at Alexandra. "She is a beauty," she agreed, running a hand over the baby, half admiring, half checking to make sure everything was as it should be.

Christine touched Alexandra's button nose and giggled to herself. How perfect it was to be holding the child that she and

Matthew had made together. A baby they could raise and watch grow into a woman who would one day love as well.

"Where is Matthew?" Christine asked.

"I sent Tom after him hours ago," Henry said. "I'll see if he has come back."

"Thank you, Henry," Isabell said, brushing a thankful hand down his arm as he walked by.

Henry went downstairs to see his messenger returning. "Tom," Henry said meeting him, "where is Matthew?"

"I went to the castle where you said he'd be," Tom spoke quickly. "They insisted he wasn't there. Hadn't been there in hours. I looked around and couldn't find him. Got a bad kind of feeling, sir."

"Come," Henry said grabbing his cloak, "I'll help find him."

Henry let Isabell know they were leaving while trying not to alarm Christine. Then he and Tom hurried off through the town asking if anyone had seen Matthew, slowly making their way back to the castle.

~

Matthew had paced the floor so long, his boots were wearing on the carpet. He had tried beating on the door to no avail, looked for any passage and realized he would have to wait until someone came for him. The sun had set; the only illumination was from the low-burning candles that flickered throughout the room. Matthew worried about Christine; she had seemed very close to having their child that morning, but she had insisted he go to the castle. His gut had told him to stay, and he was kicking himself for not listening.

Finally, the door opened, and Matthew drew his sword, prepared to fight his way out if he had to. Troy stepped in with a hard grin. "I wouldn't do that if I were you, Captain." Behind him followed five more men Matthew knew as his own. All seemed resigned and even ashamed, almost as children having to confess a grave sin to their father.

Matthew could see there was no way out. He could only pray that this was a sick joke and he would be released shortly. All hope vanished when Queen Cora stepped in provocatively wearing a sheer black gown, her hair pulled back in a tight bun on her head. "Hello, Matthew," she cooed dangerously.

"I wish I could say it is a pleasure," Matthew said through gritted teeth. "My wife is having our child; you must let me go to her."

"You know, Matthew," Cora said without a care, walking in slow circles around him as she spoke. "We could have been very happy together. You have to admit; the one time you came to my bed was life-changing. I never understood why you never returned. No matter; we could still have a chance."

"I have told you," Matthew growled. "I will never touch you again."

Cora glanced at the men behind her and gave an almost invisible nod before taking a couple of steps away from Matthew.

Moving over to Troy, she wrapped her arms around him, kissing him seductively, taking her time. As she did this, three of the other men went to grab Matthew. He raised his sword to them. "I don't want to hurt you. I am your captain; let me leave!"

"I'm sorry, Cap,'" one of the men said, "Our loyalty is to the queen."

And with that, metal hit metal in loud, ear-piercing clangs, Matthew giving everything to fight off three men at once. Matthew was strong and fast; his fight was majestic, but he was outnumbered. The men moved to surround him. He was attacked on all sides and eventually grabbed from behind. His sword was taken, but he still fought to get away with all of his strength, lifting feet off the ground with his powerful pull.

Pulling her mouth from Troy, Cora yelled, "Are you a bunch of girls?"

The soldier nearest Matthew responded with a hard blow to the captain's head, and Matthew fell to the ground unconscious.

"Remove his armor and bind his hands behind his back," Cora demanded.

The men worked quickly to obey her. Matthew groaned and turned his head a little.

"Be quick," Cora insisted.

In moments, Matthew was stripped of his armor, arms chained behind his back. Two men lifted him to his feet. Cora stood before him, grabbed his hair and pulled up his head, forcing him to face her. She slapped the side of his face. "Wake up!"

Matthew groaned again, shaking his head and slitting his eyes. He weakly tried to jerk away but was now firmly held. A million thoughts ran through his head as he tried to determine how he had ended up in this situation. What had happened? Cora had had a love/hate relationship with him for years, yet for months there had been silence. And as much as he tried, he knew there was no escape from where he found himself.

"What do you want from me?" he groaned hoarsely.

"Are you aware that your beloved is actually a queen?" Cora spit out. "Clearly trying to come in and claim my kingdom."

"What are you talking about?" Matthew said. "She is a lady, nothing more."

"Yes," Cora said. "The old man said she did not know."

"Explain your meaning," Matthew demanded. "I know nothing of this."

Cora went back to slowly pacing as she explained. "We were visited today by a man who claimed to have raised Christine. Goes by the name of David."

"Christine's father was here looking for her?"

"He raised her, but he claims he is not actually her father," Cora explained. "Says he raised her after her kingdom was destroyed. Then she ran away two years ago."

"You are wrong," Matthew said. "The man must be crazy. I am sure there is an explanation."

Ignoring him, Cora continued, "How convenient, her coming here, claiming the captain of the guard as her own, making herself a beloved in my kingdom. You expect me to think she would not overturn me? Well, try to."

"Christine and I just want to live our lives. To raise our child and live in peace. We do not want your kingdom or your throne. My life has been devoted to protecting that throne for you."

"Yes, but your loyalty only goes so far," Cora said. "If the choice was between your silly runaway queen and the Queen of Reigland, to whom you owe your loyalty, Captain, I think there is no question whom you would choose to serve."

"Christine is not a queen," Matthew insisted. "The man you spoke with must be mad, and here you are wanting to imprison me for the tales of another."

"Have you ever heard the tales of Dancé?" Cora asked, continuing to talk as if she had no care.

"The kingdom of legends," Matthew said. "It doesn't exist."

Cora laughed, "Oh, if only that were true. We were children when Dancé was overrun, so it was easy to believe it a legend. My father told me the tales. I don't know why I didn't put it together when I saw the two of you dance. The ways she moves, that damn birthmark."

Matthew was stunned silent. He was now wondering himself how he had not seen it. He put them together and still believed it to be a children's story. His wife, a queen? He had fallen in love and married a queen, and neither of them knew it? It made no sense, but Cora believed it.

"Banish us if you must," Matthew said. "We will leave and never bother you again."

"And would that not be convenient for you?" Cora scoffed. "You can run off to the little kingdom, built up an army to kill me? No. You have one way out of this and that is with me." She finally stopped pacing and moved to stand in front of him. "You still have time to make it right. Be with me, let's go back to what we once had, and we can be happy."

Cora combed her fingers through Matthew's hair and put her arms around him, but his face was hard. He said in a low hard voice, "Go back to hell you came from."

"I love it when you talk dirty," Cora said.

She took his chin in her hand and lifted his head to hers, pressing her mouth to his, begging for a passionate kiss, her body pressed into him. Anger spread through Matthew like fire. He tried to turn his head away, but she held him firm. So Matthew bit his teeth into her lip as hard as he could until he tasted blood. Cora pulled from him with a scream; wide eyes stared at him in disbelief. She wiped a hand over her lip and saw the red liquid on her fingers. She felt an awful prickle in her eyes. She was going to cry over this man she loved so passionately who loved her not at all. No, she wouldn't let anyone see her cry. She turned her hurt into rage, which flooded her entire body, and her eyes went darker than they had ever been before. She moved quickly to Troy, removed his sword from his belt, walked with cold fury back to Matthew and without a moment of thought or pause, stabbed the blade straight through his gut.

Matthew gasped for air, and all the men looked to each other in shock. Cora just stared at Matthew's wide eyes. "Wrong answer," she said in a low, angry voice.

All Matthew could see was Christine, her crystal eyes staring at him with so much love, her white hair softer than silk as he ran his fingers through it, the feel of her warm body wrapped next to his as they lay under the summer sun and her smile that lit the darkest days. She was everything; she was heaven, and he had failed her.

His weight pulled, his body falling, so the men let him drop to the ground. Cora had not moved her eyes from his face, evil searing through her like waves of fire. Troy moved across the room and squatted next to Matthew, pressing two fingers to the side of his still throat.

"He is dead," Troy said, disbelieving. Matthew had been his mentor, even his friend. Troy never imagined it would go this far. Now he saw how deep in he had gotten. "This was never part of the plan!" he rose angrily and turned to Cora.

Cora had moved quickly from rage to calm. In fact, she felt remarkably good. A sense of satisfaction, almost pleasure. She had freed herself. She cocked a half smile at her red-faced lover. "You are the captain now." She sidled over to him, ignoring the other men who knelt next to Matthew in reverence, closing his eyes and praying.

"Murder," Troy said, "this is murder in cold blood—"

Cora moved her hands up his body and wrapped her hands around his head, grabbing a lock of his hair tightly, reminding him why he needed and feared her at once. "He can't come between us anymore. I did this for you, for us." She gave his mouth a slow tantalizing kiss until he gave in to her, the poison of lust, spiked with fear, overcoming hate. She drew away from him and looked at everyone in the room. "Burn the body," she ordered. "He will receive a proper sendoff. They will believe he died tragically in the fire. Just make sure you stop it before my whole castle goes with it."

With a furious swirl, Cora was out of the room, Troy hurrying behind her.

"Where are you going?" Troy asked.

"To visit the darling queen of course," Cora said in mock sweetness. "And you are coming with me."

Troy did not argue. What was the point? He had lost Matthew and perhaps his soul; he didn't much care about the captain's wife. They wound through the castle until they retrieved their horses from the stable. They heard screams and the sound of men yelling, "Fire!

Fire!" but they did not slow, riding quickly away into the town.

~

Christine sat on the sofa with her tiny baby nestled into her

arms. Isabell had cleaned her up and brought her here to rest and wait

for Matthew's return. Christine smoothed her hand across the soft,

white hair of Alexandra's head, admiring her, then ran a thumb over

the rose-clad ankle. She thought of the stories they would tell one day,

thought of Alexandra grown and dancing at a ball like her mother,

bringing everyone to their feet. She would give her lessons right away

and would not hold her back from showing everyone her talent. She

lifted Alexandra's small hand and admired her long, dainty fingers,

thinking she might inherit her father's skill with a paintbrush. They

had an amazing life ahead of them. Nothing would ever be greater than

this moment.

There was a knock on the front door, which startled Christine

from her thoughts.

"Perhaps the men finally returned," Isabell said, moving to the

front door. "I don't know why they wouldn't just come in."

With an exasperated huff, Isabell opened the door to see Troy

and a woman covered in her cloak behind him. "Troy, what ar—" she

was cut off by the smell of something foul pressed over her mouth,

burning her lungs. The world became fuzzy, and she was gone. Troy

210

caught her body before it fell to the ground and dragged her away from the door.

"Isabell, who is it?" Christine called from the sitting room.

Cora and Troy followed the sound of her voice until they were standing before her.

"Oh, Your Majesty," Christine breathed in surprise, wanting to rise but feeling too pained from childbirth for protocol. "What a surprise."

"Have you had any visitors today?" Cora asked.

"I confess I haven't," Christine replied. "Not even my husband has returned home. To what do I owe the pleasure?"

"So you did not see a man named David?" Cora pressed.

At the sound of his name, Christine was taken back in time. She was a small child, running through green grass under a golden sun. Jack! Her brother. She was sitting in a garden with her father and mother David and Elena. Her mother—she saw her laying in a bed, her skin hot as her life slipped away. She heard the girls whispering in the library. She remembered her fight with David when he was drunk. She remembered running away—she remembered everything.

"My father," she whispered. "He was here?"

"You really don't know," Cora said in wicked victory. "The damned man was telling the truth."

"Don't know what? Is my father alright? What is going on?" Christine was panicking now.

"Your *father*, no," Cora waved a hand dismissively. "Sir David, on the other hand...well, his only ailment is a broken heart over the girl who left his protection."

"Protection, what are you saying?" Christine pressed. "If my father is here, why did you not send him?"

"To protect you, of course," Cora said with insincere concern, taking a seat beside Christine. "Sir David is not your real father; he was merely a surrogate given to you until you were old enough to learn who you really were. What kind of awful man would do that? Keeping such secrets from his queen?"

Two years she had been away. She could only imagine how worried everyone in Hanton must be. She felt a pang of guilt amongst the confusion. "I don't—what are you saying?" Christine thought back to the girls in the library. None of it made sense, and yet it all seemed to be coming together.

"Oh, what a beautiful baby," Cora gasped. "What is her name?"

"Alexandra," Christine said, taken aback by Cora's sudden interest. "She is just a couple of hours old."

"How wonderful," Cora said, her sinister tone changing to glee. "Has the captain met her?"

"He has not been home."

"Oh dear," Cora tsked. "I am sure he will return soon. There was some urgent business at the castle. May I hold her? I should like to grant your child my royal blessing."

Christine was confused and uncomfortable. Her head was swimming and Isabell had not returned to the room. "I am not sure that is such a good idea. I just got her to sleep."

"Oh please, darling," Cora pressed. "It would mean so much."

Cora took Alexandra from Christine's arms without waiting for permission. As Christine tried to figure out what was going on, Troy drew his sword. Christine panicked, "No!" rising to reach for her daughter, but Troy slid his sword under her ribs and pierced her heart. She fell back into the chair.

"You will not wear a crown; you will not steal my throne, and you will not lord Matthew's admiration for you over me anymore," Cora spit. "This baby should have been mine, and because you stole her, I will send her to be raised by maids. She will never know you or her father or what it feels like to be free. She will spend her days working for me, never allowed to go outside or fall in love. She will live out your sentence until her death." This was Cora's last curse upon Matthew and Christine, and it landed upon the life of baby Alexandra.

Christine's eyes closed, her life gone. Troy was already moving to knock over candles and lamps, sofas and curtains beginning to rise in flames.

"We have to go," Troy said, taking Cora by the arm and leading her from the house. He put her in the back of the carriage with Alexandra and had the horse moving in seconds. He felt dead inside. *When did I become her monster?*

Henry was riding back, hoping that Matthew had somehow crossed his path and returned home. When he was close, he noticed the flames breaking through the side windows. Panic swept through him, and he kicked his heels into his horse, in a mad race for the house. He pulled to a stop so hard, the horse almost turned over. Dropping to his feet, Henry burst through the front door. "Isabell!"

He heard a cough and saw Isabell lying on the floor surrounded by thick, black smoke. Everything was burning, the walls, the staircase, the doors; it was all orange, red and hot. "Isabell," Henry dropped next to his wife, lifted her into his arms and ran out the front door with her, the roof caving in and crashing the moment they hit the dirt. Henry dropped to the ground, laying Isabell flat. "Breathe," Henry begged.

Isabell gasped for air, her body covered in soot, but she was not burned.

"Christine," she gasped out.

Henry looked up at the house, flames rising to the sky, every inch taken by fire. Isabell forced her eyes to look as well, and they both knew. Isabell gripped Henry's shirt, and he pulled her into him. Isabell sobbed, and tears fell down Henry's stunned face. They were gone. Christine, the baby. The sick feeling in his gut told Henry Matthew was gone too.

Chapter Sixteen

So Long My Love

In the lowest corridor of the castle, Bessie sat at her desk that was piled in silks and tulle, her needle-pricked fingers sewing intricate patterns down the seam of what would be Queen Cora's gown. Bessie's gowns were perfect; she was the only one Cora permitted to make her gowns, and Bessie worked tirelessly day and night.

Caramel blonde hair was pulled into a full, long ponytail, though some strands had fallen loose, and pale skin showed how little she was exposed to the sun. The room she worked in was large, the walls lined with racks of fabric and materials. Through a back door was the small room where she slept.

A loud creak brought Bessie out of her trance. She looked up from her work to see three guards walk in followed by Queen Cora. Bessie rose quickly to her feet, laying her spectacles on the table and giving a deep curtsy. "Your Majesty," she said, "to what do I owe this unusual surprise?"

It was then Bessie noticed the baby wrapped warmly in a blanket held by one of the Queen's men. "I want you to take this child," Cora told her. "Keep her here and raise her."

"Who is she?" Bessie asked.

"You will not ask who or where she came from," Cora continued. "The maids will help you raise her. When she is old enough, you will train her to work with you. And most importantly, you will never let her roam past the servants' hall and kitchen."

"Is she the daughter of a prisoner?" Bessie questioned.

"Her parents are dead," Cora spoke coldly. "She will serve the sentence they couldn't. Her name is Alexandra."

Cora flicked two fingers, and the man brought Alexandra to Bessie, handing her over to her care.

"No more questions," Cora demanded. "And you will keep your mouth shut. She is your child. And if you disobey any of the instructions I have given you, it won't just be your job; it will be your head and the baby's life. Killing an innocent child is even low for my taste, so do as I say."

Bessie curtsied in acceptance and looked down at the small bundle in her arms. The baby could not have been more than a couple of days old, so small and frail. She would have to find a wet nurse to feed her, and she would sew dresses for her. Bessie had never married, her whole life devoted to serving Cora, and she never dreamed she would ever have a child. As heartbreaking as she imagined the circumstances that brought the baby to her might be, she would raise her with all the love she had.

"Alexandra," she cooed softly, running a thin finger down the side of the baby's cheek after the queen and her men had left.

Alexandra's tiny feet escaped the blanket, and a small, pink mark caught Bessie's attention. She looked closer to see the rose birthmark on the baby's ankle. "Where did you come from?"

~

A few days later Henry and Isabell were by the sea setting a memorial for their friends who had been stolen from them far too soon: a wooden cross surrounded by grey stones and flowers. The cross read:

Captain Matthew and Lady Christine of Reigland

Alexandra.

Loved for moments, remembered forever

Henry put his arm around Isabell, the wind whipping through their hair. They stood silently with their memories, their heartbreak and the sound of the sea. Henry had made some inquiries at the castle about Matthew and was told Matthew had passed in a tragic fire. Henry and Isabell knew better, and the note had been ripped and thrown into the sea. Their life had been far too quiet in the days that followed the murders. They finally had to accept where they stood and set the memorial.

"What do we do now?" Isabell asked from beneath Henry's arm. "The queen of our kingdom has them killed—the person we trust to rule and protect."

"Which means there is nothing we can do," Henry said. "If we go to anyone in the castle, it will be our heads as well."

"Should we leave?" Isabell asked.

"And go where, my love?" Henry asked gently. "Our home, our livelihood, it is all here. People rely on us to provide care."

"And when the king's men come to me for medical attention," Isabell asked, "I am supposed to support their bodies in the healing they took from Matthew and Christine—from Alexandra?" They believed Alexandra died with Christine in the fire.

Henry was silent, holding her close. It was an impossible position.

"They are fools if they seek help from us now," Henry stated. "They are not simple enough to think we do not know what they did. They will fear putting their lives in our hands."

"I can't stay here," Isabell said through tears. "But I cannot leave. I want to storm the court and kill them all. I cannot sleep, but I am always tired. It is an impossible place to be. My body is weakening with every passing day. How can I go on?"

Henry turned Isabell to face him, putting his hands on her shoulders and forcing her to look at him. "You go on because you must," he told her. "Because I need you. Because the children and mothers and fathers of Reigland need you. Because no matter how bad it gets, there is always a reason to keep going. Another day on the horizon. I don't know why Matthew and Christine were taken from us, but I do know there is a reason we are still here. We cannot give up. We won't."

Isabell wrapped her arms around Henry, squeezing her face tight into his chest and let every tear fall. Henry brushed his hand down her hair, comforting her as best he could, his own heart shattered.

"You are not alone," he told her. "I am here and will not leave you."

Isabell nodded into his chest, unable to speak.

They did go on, as impossible as it felt; they survived. The days got easier, though they never forgot the ones they lost. An empty spot always remained, but they found a way to love each other and do their work. No one knew exactly what happened to Captain Matthew and his wife. Matthew's death was ruled a tragic accident, but Christine was never acknowledged by the queen. Rumors spread that she had returned to where she had come from. Others wondered if she had died in childbirth. Knowing what they did, Henry and Isabell refused to speak of it to anyone, clinging closely to each other.

They had no reason to believe Alexandra was alive. After all, she must have died in the fire with Christine. There was nothing to hint that she was growing up in the belly of the castle as an orphan.

~

David returned to Hanton with a heavy heart. He had spent years searching and hoping Christine would find her way home. He now had to resign himself to the fact she was likely gone. His body had grown old in that time, though he was not yet fifty. He was destroyed from the inside out.

When he entered the castle, Jack was there to meet him. "Father, you've come home."

Jack was a grown man now. He had worked closely with Thomas for over a year, assisting him with anything required. Jack missed Christine, but he had settled into his life and responsibilities in Hanton.

Every time David came home, there was a spark of hope that immediately died. Jack knew his sister would not come back, but that did not stop the spike of his heart. Some part deep inside him that always seemed to betray.

"I won't go back again," David said firmly, removing his cloak and hat, handing them to the waiting hand. "I have searched far and wide. I've returned and asked again—she is gone."

Jack was not surprised. He had tried to talk his father into staying the year before, but his duty to Dancé had kept him going. That did not change the weight of his father actually saying it. Saying she was gone for good, beloved Christine.

His father looked old, hair grey from stress, face wrinkled. He was thin, frail and weak. Every year of hunting and worry showed.

"I will stay," David told Jack. "I will not leave and just pray every day that she returns. I realize too that in my desperate chase to find someone who doesn't want to be found, I have neglected the one person I have left. You are a grown man now, but you are still my son. I want to know you."

Jack nodded simply and said, "I would like that."

Thomas had never been the same. All the life left inside him vanished with Christine. A few short months after she had run away, Thomas had married a princess, a marriage his father arranged. Thomas did not want to, but his duty to Hanton demanded he marry and provide a son to rule.

Within a year she did give him an heir. This pleased the king, and Thomas loved the boy, but he couldn't feel the joy he ought to. So much of his life had been devoted to Dancé, only for his faithful quest to be for naught. He had become a very quiet man. No one had seen him smile since the day he and Christine had danced. Though he was kind to his wife and children, his life was one of a mourner.

Thomas's wife was Diana, a kind, elegant woman who filled her role perfectly. Over the years of their marriage, she knew a certain love had grown between them, though it was nothing you would find in fairytales. She did not know what haunted her husband, only that he was haunted, and that would never change. She would wake in the night to him fighting the bed in his sleep or calling out to the darkness. She would sooth him as best she could, her gentle arms pulling him back to peace. She gave him all she had but knew it wasn't enough— and the nightmares always returned.

All hope seemed lost forever.

Chapter Seventeen

Seamstress to the Queen

Eighteen Years Later

The sun rose over Reigland, sending rays of light through the small window in Alexandra's room. Opening her eyes, she yawned and stretched the night's sleep from her body. Her room was little more than an alcove off Bessie's room, a bed and small dresser her only furniture. Alexandra was tall and thin. Her fine white-blonde hair fell around her shoulders; her eyes were the most crystalline blue any of the queen's staff had ever seen. She lived in the cellars below the castle, never allowed to leave under any circumstances. She wanted to see the world, to know the feeling of grass beneath her bare feet and taste the sea air Bessie spoke of. But her world was restricted to the cold belly of the castle. And though those around her treated her kindly, a single step beyond her boundaries meant severe punishment.

Alexandra rose from her bed, washed and dressed before making her way to the large kitchen for breakfast. The kitchen was swarmed with cooks and servants, making food and taking it to those who resided in the castle. Alexandra perched herself on a stool in front of a bar which overlooked the whole kitchen. "Good morning," she called cheerfully.

"Our sleeping beauty awakes," Chef Roland called. "About time you got up."

Alexandra giggled. She was their girl; all of the servants loved her. No one knew where she came from, only that she had been brought to them as a baby. Together they had raised her, caring for and protecting her.

Layla, daughter of Chef Roland and Alexandra's closest friend, came and sat next to Alexandra. "Good morning, Alexandra," she greeted. "You almost missed breakfast."

"Why didn't you wake me?" Alexandra asked.

"You know Father. If a lady sleeps, then she must need it."

Two plates with eggs, sausage, sliced fruits and a hot biscuit were placed before Alexandra and Layla.

"Thank you," Alexandra said.

"Will you be with Bessie again today?" Layla asked.

"Yes," Alexandra replied. "With the queen's birthday ball on the horizon, there is extra work."

"And Bessie won't let anyone but you help her," Layla added.

"Bessie knows what she wants," Alexandra said. "And after all the time she has spent with me, I am the closest she can get to her own hands."

"I do not envy you," Layla said. "You see the queen today?"

"Yes, we are doing her fitting."

"Your first time seeing the queen," Layla said. "That is exciting."

"I would rather see something outside of this place," Alexandra said. "But I'll settle for going upstairs. I'm excited, but also a little frightened."

"I still do not understand that," Layla told her. "What could it hurt if you went outside? Perhaps you are the daughter of a fugitive."

"What an awful thought," Alexandra said in a high-pitched tone. "I prefer to think of my parents in a more romantic light."

"Bastard of the king?" Layla asked.

"Not hardly," Alexandra rejected, taking a large bite of biscuit.

"It could be whatever you want," Layla conceded. "There is something romantic about not knowing where you came from. You can make your story whatever you like, and no one will say otherwise."

"Lost, more like," Alexandra said. "I am eighteen years old; I know there should be more to my life than this. I'm a prisoner living out the sentence of a crime I never stood trial for."

Layla was silent. She knew Alexandra was right. They had been friends for years, but their friendship was confined to the castle walls. Neither understood why Layla could go anywhere she liked, but Alexandra was kept inside. It limited their friendship.

"I was thinking of trying to sneak out," Alexandra whispered. "Just for a little while."

Layla choked on her tea. "You know what happens when you get caught snooping where you don't belong," she said.

"No one will know this time," Alexandra defended. "You could go with me. We will do it late at night and be back before anyone notices."

"I don't know," Layla said cautiously.

"What would happen if I was caught?" Alexandra asked. "I'd be flogged? Again. At this point, I don't care. I will go crazy if I never go out, at least for a little while."

"The last time you tried to leave you were locked in the cellar without food for days," Layla reminded.

"I cannot just sit around here and decay into the Queen's dresses," Alexandra said.

Layla thought for a minute. "I know a passage," she said. "We could try."

"Tonight?" Alexandra pressed.

"Why so soon?" Layla asked in exasperation. "You are talking about going against the queen's orders; that is no small thing."

"It is not soon," Alexandra objected. "It is eighteen years too long."

"I know," Layla conceded. "Don't breathe a word to anyone."

Alexandra smiled and returned her focus to breakfast.

Bessie walked in just a few minutes later. "Alexandra," she called, "we have to get moving."

"I'll see you tonight," Alexandra hugged her friend. Hopping off the stool, she followed Bessie out of the room.

They entered the large room where all the sewing was done. "I have everything we will need right here," Bessie pointed out a pile of fabrics and measuring tools. "Help me gather it up, and we can go."

Alexandra's heart beat fast, her stomach filling with a million butterflies. She had never gone beyond the servant hall, and now she was going to help fit the queen! She took deep breaths, pulling herself together and helped collect the items Bessie had laid out.

When they were ready, Alexandra followed Bessie out of the room and down a hall she had never seen. At the end of the hall were stairs. Bessie stopped and turned to Alexandra. "You will not open your mouth; you will not even look Her Majesty in the eye. If you screw up, you may never be allowed up here again. It is not my decision; I am following orders from the queen. Do you understand?"

"Yes, ma'am," Alexandra said, her skin paler than ever.

They went through a door, and the whole world changed. Wooden walls were replaced with scarlet, torches turned from black metal to gold. Not a single scuff on the walls or speck on the carpets. Alexandra felt she had stepped into a dream. Her eyes wandered over the lavish rooms.

Uniformed guards stood tall at every doorway, the sight of them frightening. She had seen some of the queen's guard a few times over the years, but not like this. Their backs straight as wood, their eyes stone, looking off to the distance, never moving.

Alexandra followed Bessie until they reached a well-appointed room. Walls covered in red and black striped silk, flowers in tall crystal vases, three tall gold-framed mirrors standing together before a round platform, and a glittering chandelier hanging from the ceiling, sending colored spangles of lights across the dark walls. Alexandra turned in slow circles, looking at everything in amazement. "This place is incredible."

"Don't touch anything," Bessie warned as she arranged what was needed.

Alexandra's attention was drawn to a window, five times the size of her own. Walking timidly over, she placed her hands on the sill, which was cold to her palms. Her eyes were dazzled by the bright sun, then adjusted to the scene before her. The world was bigger than she ever could have imagined. Horses and people spread like pepper over a manicured lawn. Beyond it, gates and roads, homes and towers. Further on, hills of green and a sky of brilliant blue. Alexandra felt invincible. She wondered if she could jump, or maybe even fly. The whole world was right there in front of her, calling, begging her to take it.

Two doors swung open with a bang, startling Alexandra. Her heart skipped as she spun to see two guards holding the doors and bowing low as a tall, thin woman came in. She wore a corset and knee highs, a sheer robe draped over her shoulders. Alexandra thought she was the most frighteningly beautiful woman she had ever seen. Her eyes were expertly painted, her lips blood red and her hair, black as night, spilling around her shoulders and down her bodice. She knew it must be the queen. Three handmaids rushed in behind her, skittish, with faces like scorned children.

"Your Majesty," Bessie bowed at Cora who sat on a couch and swung one long leg over the other.

"Let's get this done," Cora said in a voice as haughty as the way she held her head. She looked idly at her painted nails and waited.

"Yes, Majesty." Bessie scurried over to her things and gave an anxious wave for Alexandra to come help.

Nervous, Alexandra hurried to Bessie and helped lift fabrics of different colors and types. "Have you decided what color you will be wearing?" Bessie asked breathlessly.

Cora lifted her eyes, a piercing stare trailing along the fabrics held before her. Then she locked eyes with Alexandra, who shook and quit breathing under her gaze. Cora was equally startled, thinking at first she saw a ghost. Alexandra had her mother's perfect hair and crystal eyes, though her small frame came across more timidly, she was the spitting image of her mother.

Cora's eyes moved back to Bessie. "What is she doing here?" she asked coldly.

"Beg pardon, Your Majesty," Bessie stuttered. "There is a great deal of work in preparation for your ball. I didn't think the girl helping me would cause harm. She's still in the castle. We will return right back to our quarters when we have completed your measurements."

Cora rose slowly to her feet, seeming ten feet tall to Alexandra, who gulped in fear.

"I gave clear instructions," Cora said to Bessie. "And you betrayed me."

"Your Majesty, please—" Bessie began, but Cora lifted her hand to silence her.

"Do not even try," Cora said coldly before turning to her guards. "Take her."

Bessie began to panic, "No, please, Majesty!" She threw herself to Cora's feet. "I will do anything. Please, I did not mean to disobey you."

The guards lifted Bessie's kicking, frantic body from the ground and dragged her out. Alexandra called out, "No! Where are you taking her?" She tried to fight off one of the guards who threw her to the ground. The door was slammed shut and Alexandra was left beating on it, locked from the outside, "No! Please, don't take her, it was my fault!" she turned her attention back to Cora, tears falling from her eyes, "Please Your Majesty, it was my fault."

"What is your name?" Cora asked as Bessie's screams faded. Cora knew her name of course. No matter how many times she tried to forget the girl in the basement, she couldn't. She

"Alexandra," she said wiping tears from her eyes. "What will happen to her?"

Cora looked Alexandra up and down critically, walking around her in slow, tight circles. "Has Bessie taught you well? Taken care of you?"

"Yes, ma'am—I mean Your Majesty," Alexandra bowed her head. "I am the only one she trusts to assist her."

"Good," Cora said. "Because you will be doing her job."

Alexandra shook. "What will happen to Bessie?" she asked.

Cora stepped up to the round stand in front of the mirrors. "Don't worry about Bessie, dear. I want a green gown of silk with black lace. Can you do that?"

Cora was not going to give Alexandra the answer she wanted and she knew it. Alexandra could scream and fight, but she had been through enough punishment to know it would never help anything. Taking deep breathes, Alexandra forced herself into survival mode. "Yes," Alexandra said. "Whatever you like, My Queen."

Cora gave a smile that sent shivers through Alexandra's spine. Cora examined herself in the three mirrors, turning and rubbing hands down her bodice in admiration. She was beautiful and frightening. Her confidence could make an entire room turn to ice, and her stare made

Alexandra want to hide under a table like a small child during a thunderstorm.

"Do you like what you see, Alexandra?" Cora asked coolly.

Alexandra stuttered, "Yes—er, no, ma'am—Majesty—I just, I have never seen a woman like you before."

Cora smiled and stepped down to where she was standing in front of the wide-eyed Alexandra. "And what kind of woman would that be?" She ran a cold finger down the side of Alexandra's cheek.

"I don't mean anything bad," Alexandra defended anxiously. "I just mean, you are so beautiful, and your clothes are magnificent."

Cora cocked her head and narrowed her eyes. Seemingly satisfied, she returned to the platform. "I am your canvas now," Cora said. "Amaze me."

Alexandra's fingers shook as she measured and pinned. "You must be excited for your birthday."

"The help does not normally talk," Cora scolded.

"Sorry," Alexandra whispered and renewed her focus. She tried not to think about Bessie, fighting off the tears that continued to escape her eyes. She had never been more terrified in her life and was now completely alone.

"I am excited for my ball," Cora said, admiring herself. "You cannot imagine how wonderful it feels when everyone fawns over you."

"I should like to see a ball one day," Alexandra said.

Cora laughed in mockery. "You? Oh, my dear child, the last place you will ever find yourself is at a ball in my castle."

Alexandra lowered her eyes and focused silently until she had completed her task. When she was done, one of the handmaids helped Alexandra take her things back to the sewing room. Alexandra set the dress to be sewn on the stand and turned to the shy girl. "When will Bessie be coming back?"

The girl would not meet Alexandra's eyes. "She won't, ma'am. When you have displeased the queen, you never come back."

"But how did Bessie displease her?" Alexandra asked. "She did not do anything wrong."

"She brought you," the girl whispered.

"Me? Well, of course, she needed my help."

"Majesty refuses to let you leave," the girl said.

"But why?" Alexandra asked. "What is so important about me that I cannot leave these cold walls? What could I have ever done to her, I've been here since I was born!"

"I don't know," the girl admitted. "She demands it, though. And when the queen demands, you do not question."

The girl turned and hurried away.

"Wait," Alexandra called. "I don't understand."

But the girl was already gone.

Now alone, the adrenaline that brought her this far left her body and Alexandra fell to the floor with violent sobs. Bessie had cared for her as long as she could remember. Every day was spent working side by side. She couldn't grasp what had just transpired, but it destroyed everything inside her.

It was after nightfall when Alexandra had cried her tears and composed herself enough to turn her attention to the dark green dress on the stand, so lonely without someone to wear it. She ran her hand down the smooth silk and examined the black lace along the top. She imagined how it would look completed and regretted she would never see it worn to a ball.

Grabbing the pin in her hair, she shook her long locks around her shoulders and closed her eyes. She imagined herself in a room, rich as the one she had just seen, but full of people dressed in fine clothes. She saw a man, young and handsome, come and ask her to dance. Without realizing what she was doing, she began to dance in the room by herself, turning and swaying, whisked away by the music in her mind. When she returned to reality, her eyes opened to the pile of discarded fabrics that were not the queen's liking. A smile spread across her face with an idea, but she would have to finish the queen's dress first. Without another second of delay, Alexandra went to work.

~

After a soft knock on the door, Layla entering the sewing room. A couple of lamps lit the room since night had fallen. Alexandra was on the floor against the wall, staring at her needle-pricked fingers. She looked weak and tired. On the nearby stand was the most beautiful dress Layla had ever seen. She walked over and ran her finger along the side. The dress was green strapless with sheer, black lace along the top creating accented sleeves. The bodice was small and the skirt would hug the queen's slim figure, a lace train falling down the back.

"Do you think the queen will approve?" Alexandra asked without looking up from her hands.

"It's the most beautiful work you or Bessie has ever done," Layla said, moving to sit beside her friend.

"Bessie would punish me for how provocative the bodice is," Alexandra said. "After seeing the queen today, it seems just what she would want."

"I think she will like it," Layla assured.

After a silence, Alexandra said, "She's dead, isn't she?"

Layla knew what she meant, and it made her sick. But she couldn't say the words out loud. Her silence was enough of an answer.

"I don't understand," Alexandra said as tears began to fall down her face. "All she did was ask for help. How is that so wrong?"

Layla wrapped her arms around Alexandra who leaned into them and wept. "I don't know." Layla stroked her hair silently. She had no other answers. The way Queen Cora felt about Alexandra made no sense. But then, everyone knew that nothing Cora wanted made sense. It was just law.

A while later when Alexandra had cried her tears, she sat up and wiped her face. "I am going to that ball," she said.

Chapter Eighteen

A Night to Remember

The Queen of Reigland demanded nothing short of everything, and this on a normal day. On the day of her birthday, the castle was pure chaos. Extra hands were brought in to help cook and prepare, and the guards were in a panic over the vast guest list.

Cora sat before her mirror, staring at her reflection. There was a hollow within her that was never acknowledged, but she had caught her own eye and was lost. She did not recognize herself anymore. Her terrifying eyes held sadness she could no longer disguise. But when there was a knock at the door, she hardened herself again. "Come in."

She rose and moved to sit on the edge of her bed as Prince Alabe walked in. "Hello, My Queen wife," he said.

"Alabe," she cooed sweetly. "To what do I owe this surprise?"

"I have brought a gift for you," he said, moving close to her.

Over the last years, she and Alabe had grown rather cordial. Though she did not entertain him often, a truce had developed between them. In some strange way, they had a twisted love for each other which would never be acknowledged.

Cora waited patiently with a smile as Alabe moved to sit beside her. He revealed a square box of black suede and opened it. Cora gasped when she saw the golden necklace with black stones. "It is the most beautiful thing anyone has ever given me," Cora said. For a moment Alabe thought he saw the glisten of a tear, but it was blinked back and forgotten.

"May I?" Alabe asked, lifting the necklace from its box.

Cora turned her back to him and moved her hair to the side. She felt the thick, cold jewelry fall against her neck, lying perfectly on her chest. She lifted the end and stared at it. When Alabe had fastened it, he leaned down and kissed her shoulder. "Happy birthday," he said.

Cora turned and looked into the eyes of her husband the king. She knew the smallest drop of a pebble would break the dam within her, but she would not let it. An ache within her wanted to admit that she loved Alabe, but that too did not fit her, and she swallowed it down.

Alabe saw her weakness and pulled her into him, brushing his lips softly over hers. Her body became weak, and she fell into his touch, kissing passionately. Her walls were down, and she gave into him, every bit of her.

~

Alexandra looked at herself in the small, cracked mirror. She had sewn herself a dress of purple, her favorite color. It was the most beautiful thing she had ever put on her body, with a shaped bodice and a skirt that flowed loosely around her legs. Layla had given her silver slippers, and she wore the mask over her eyes. She did not recognize herself, and she loved it. She didn't want to be Alexandra, the seamstress, the cellar mouse, anymore.

Layla was far too afraid to go with her, but she told Alexandra about a back passage. Gathering her skirts, Alexandra crept quietly to the secret door. She opened it to find a low illuminated chamber. The sound of music and chatter could be heard in a murmur through the wall. When she opened the door, everything came to life. Men in suits, women with pearls around their necks and jewels in their hair, all chattering and laughing. Alexandra was so stunned she could barely take it all in. The ceiling so high and room so large, she imagined everyone in the world was stuffed into the room.

She realized now that her hands were cold and sweating. Touching her mask to ensure her face was well covered, she moved through the crowd around the edge of the room. No one seemed to notice her; she was just another guest. She took in everything, eavesdropping on men and woman speaking of ungodly things, groups of women admiring handsome gentlemen and mocking the ladies they didn't approve of. None of it made sense to her; she was dizzy with all the color, the variety, the strange people, but she was enchanted by it all, nonetheless.

"Wine, madam?"

Alexandra froze at the sight of a servant offering her wine. She had seen him a few times before. She feared he would recognize her.

So without saying a word, she took a glass and bowed her head in thanks. The man went on without a care.

Alexandra sipped on the sweet wine, and the dance floor caught her eye. For a good while she stood there in awe watching men turn women around the floor, their skirts flying around them. She did not notice her body begin to sway with the music.

"Some party," a male voice said behind her.

Alexandra turned sharply to see a tall man looking right at her. He smiled at her, a broad, handsome smile, blue eyes gazing and shaggy brown hair falling from beneath a crown. He was royalty. Alexandra's heart stopped; she feared he was the King of Reigland and would have her dragged off and killed. But his eyes did not seem angry or cruel; they looked kind and gentle. He was also very young, about her age. She thought he might be a prince.

Alexandra bent into a curtsy. "Your Majesty."

"Please," he said taking her hand and pulling her back to her feet. "Call me Tommy."

"Tommy?" Alexandra asked. "That does not sound like a royal name."

"Short for Thomas," the man explained. "I am the second; Prince Thomas is my father. To avoid confusion, people call me Tommy. My father hates it; he thinks a man should own his name. He is probably right. Please, what is your name, sweet maiden?"

Alexandra blushed. "Alexandra."

"Lady Alexandra," the prince took her hand and kissed it. "And why do you wear a mask when this is not a masquerade?"

"To be honest with you, sir," she said, "I was not exactly invited."

Tommy laughed. "Oh, I like you already. Please," he took her glass and handed it with his own to the man standing behind him who seemed to be his servant. Then he bowed and put out a hand to Alexandra. "May I have the honor of the next dance?"

Dance? With all these people watching? Alexandra loved dancing in her room, but she had never danced with a man before. Surely, they would draw attention and then the queen would see Alexandra had disobeyed. On the other hand, this might be her only chance to dance with a Prince, especially at a ball. She had come this far, and if she turned back now, she would regret it for the rest of her life. So placing a shaky hand into his, she said, "I would be honored."

Tommy's hand was large compared to hers and strong. His skin dark from sun. Yet somehow, the way his hand wrapped around hers, Alexandra felt safe. Something about his touch gave her hope and filled her with butterflies.

A song had just ended, and everyone was walking off the dance floor when Tommy and Alexandra stepped out. Alexandra turned back at the people clearing and asked nervously, "Perhaps the dancing has ended?"

"The party has just begun," Tommy said, pulling her into him. "It is our turn."

Tommy was a head taller than Alexandra. She tilted her head to see his face. His entire stance was that of confidence, and he looked at her with a sparkle in his eye. Her heart thumped loudly against him, but she did not run away. She did not want to run away. As dangerous as this had become, it was thrilling.

At the end of the room, Cora noticed Prince Thomas II on the dance floor with a girl she did not recognize. "Who is that?" she asked. There was something familiar about her that made her gut turn.

"I do not know," the man near her had to admit. "I have never seen her before."

"Why does she wear a mask?" Alabe asked from beside Cora.

"Clearly she has something to hide," Cora said. "When the dance is over, I want you to have her discreetly escorted out and questioned."

"Yes, Your Majesty," the man said.

A single note and the dance had begun. Alexandra thought she was going to be sick with nerves until the music started and a calm came over her she'd never felt before. And when the prince began to move, Alexandra moved with him in perfect harmony. They moved in swift turns and bends. He spun her around, and when she stopped, he lifted her in the air, and her leg kicked out with ethereal grace.

Cora's blood went cold when she saw the rose birthmark on the side of the girl's ankle. She gripped Alabe's leg so tight, he thought her nails would draw blood. "My Queen, what is it?" he asked in concern.

"It's her."

"Her who? What are you talking about? And for the love of the crown, release my leg."

Cora turned and saw how she clung to him. Releasing his leg, she straightened her back and said, "That servant girl. The daughter of that witch Christine."

"Daughter?" Alabe asked, more confused than ever. "I thought they were dead."

"They had a child," Cora said. "I let her live in the servants keep with that seamstress woman. I should have killed her years ago."

Cora turned to the man behind her and said, "Forget discreet. When the dance ends, arrest her."

The man bowed and went to inform the guards of her instructions.

"I do not think a scene is what you want," Alabe warned.

"You have found my good graces," Cora hissed. "Don't throw that away over a stupid girl, or I'll have your head as well."

As the music came to an end, Alexandra felt perfect. She had entered heaven and flown through the clouds. She felt untouchable. She and the prince were lost in each other. Then something caught

Tommy's attention. There was a look of confusion on his face. Alexandra followed his gaze to see five guards coming straight for her. She went pale.

"What is this?" Prince Thomas demanded.

"I beg your pardon, Prince Thomas," one of the men said. "We are to arrest her."

"No, please!" Alexandra begged as two guards wrenched her from the arms of the prince. "Please don't, I am sorry, I won't do it again, please!"

"Stop," Tommy ordered. "Do not take her."

"My dear prince," Cora said coolly, coming to stand before him. "I am sorry you were tricked. This woman is a servant in my castle, forbidden from leaving the servants' quarters. I assure you, the punishment will be just."

Alexandra was crying now, her whole little world in flames, the guards holding her so tightly she thought her arms might break.

Cora turned to walk away when Tommy called, "Wait! If this girl is causing you so much hardship, send her with me."

Cora laughed and turned back to him. "Are you mad? This girl is of no use to you. She is going to be disposed of."

"You have no use for her then," Tommy pressed. "Let me take her."

Alexandra was frozen. She could not breathe watching the queen and prince fight over her very life. The entire room was quiet, watching closely to see what would happen.

"She is a worthless maid," Cora hissed. "Why do you want her so bad?"

"You speak as if she is nothing, yet you fight for her like your own life. What is it about this girl that frightens you?"

Cora's mouth clamped shut. She turned to see every eye in the room staring at them. Taking a step back, she inhaled a deep breath. "Fine," she said. "But don't ever bring her back here."

The men released Alexandra, and she fell to the floor, her body giving out. Tommy moved over to her quickly, the man that was with him hurrying over as well. Alexandra was gasping for air. "It is alright," he assured her, "you are safe."

The men helped her up. Giving Cora no time to change her mind, they hurried from the room. Alabe came behind Cora. "You are letting her go?"

The music started up, and the guests returned to mingling as though nothing had happened.

"They will not make it back to Hanton," she said before turning and walking back to her men. "Wait until they have left the city. Then hunt them down and kill them. All of them. Make sure you leave no evidence of any kind. That is a king's grandson."

The man nodded to Cora and he and his men were gone.

"He's a prince?" Layla gasped in amazement.

Alexandra gave a nervous giggle. "I know; my head is spinning. We have to leave immediately; the queen is after my head."

Tommy and his man had gone with Alexandra at her desperate request to tell her friend goodbye. They urged her to be quick; Queen Cora was known to not let things go until she saw blood.

There were tears welling in Layla's eyes. "I am going to miss you, but I am so happy. Go, live a real life."

"I will," Alexandra hugged her friend.

"What will he do with you?" Layla asked.

"I don't know," Alexandra told her honestly. "He may let me work in his castle. I will do anything for him if it means out of here."

"Be safe," Layla said, squeezing her arm.

"You too. I won't forget you."

"I am sorry, but we have to go," the prince said, coming behind Alexandra and gently taking her elbow.

The girls gave one last smile to each other. Layla squeezed Alexandra's arms reassuringly, and Alexandra let the handsome prince lead her out of the castle.

Alexandra was in a swarm of emotions, having no time to take in what was happening. Most of her had known that sneaking to the ball would cost her head, but she had been so angry and she had gone—and now she was being escorted away by a prince from another land!

Many of Cora's men gave astonished looks to Alexandra as they headed for the front door. Alexandra kept her head down and body close to the prince who still held her arm. Hearts beating fast, they didn't slow down until they were on the wide front steps. Alexandra froze.

A cool whiff of evening air hit her whole body, and she shivered, eyes scanning the manicured lawn and then looking up at the sky of diamonds. She was frozen, shaking with fear—and thrill!

"My Lady Alexandra," Tommy said trying to return her attention. He had stopped with her and was desperate to get moving again.

Alexandra just stared up at the sky. "I've never been outside before," she nearly whispered.

The prince looked at his man who returned his gaze in understanding. They both experienced a flare of anger that anyone would be restricted from any freedom for their entire life. It was unfathomable. A sentence worse than death.

The prince stood in front of her and drew her gaze back to his. "I swear on my life and my crown, you will never be locked away again. But for now, we have to go. Her Majesty is not not forgiving and very enraged by us taking you; we need to return to Hanton as quickly as possible."

Alexandra gave a shaky nod and let Tommy lead her down the steps and into the waiting carriage. Soldiers on horseback rode in front and behind them on black stallions. The moment Tommy and Alexandra were in the carriage, they were moving.

Tommy sat beside Alexandra, looking out the window, hoping no one would chase after them. Alexandra sat uncomfortably, unsure of how to act and keenly aware she was alone with a man. Taking deep breaths, she tried to center herself and come to terms with everything that had happened. But how could she? Her whole life had been within restricted walls, believing herself hated by everyone on the outside. Now the woman who had been like a mother was dead, and she was running away with a prince she did not know. She inhaled deeply and exhaled slowly.

"Are you alright?" Tommy asked, resting a gentle hand on hers.

Alexandra stared down at where his hand touched her. She liked it. "I think I am," she said. "To be honest with you; I am not sure yet. Everything is happening so fast—I'm frightened."

"It did not seem we had much choice," Tommy told her. "I think Her Majesty was after your head."

"She was," Alexandra whispered in shame.

"Why?" Tommy asked. "Forgive me, but who are you to her that she would be so angry toward your existence."

"To be honest with you, I don't even know," Alexandra told him. "I was raised by the servants, who were all kind to me. The seamstress Bessie was in charge of my care. She said I was brought to her as a baby, but no one knew where I came from or why the queen brought me to them."

"You were given to the servants by the queen as an infant?" Tommy asked.

"That is what I was told," Alexandra said. "That, and she ordered I was never to leave. I could go from our rooms to the kitchen, no further. I never knew why. But two days ago, Bessie took me to help her fit the queen for her birthday gown. When the queen saw me outside of the servants' hall—" Alexandra choked on tears. "She had Bessie taken away and killed. I swear, Your Majesty, I do not know where I came from or why the queen feels this way about me."

The prince listened to her story in astonishment. He knew she was telling the truth. What he could not understand was why. Why the queen would take a baby and hide her away from the world, and why as a grown woman, she would keep her hidden.

"You are safe now," Tommy said gently.

Alexandra nodded, sniffing away tears. Tommy cupped his hand over her cheek and turned her to him. "May I?" he asked, reaching for the tie on her mask.

Alexandra nodded. Tommy tugged at the perfect bow, releasing its hold, then slowly removed the silver mask from her face.

His heart stopped. He did not understand it, but she was the most beautiful woman he had ever seen with her white-blond hair and eyes of the most enchanting crystal blue. Her skin was so light, but her cheeks flushed pink. The way she looked into his eyes enthralled him. For a minute they just stared at each other, breath mingling from their proximity.

"You are beautiful," Tommy said quietly.

"Thank you, Majesty," she replied.

"Tommy."

"Tommy."

He wanted to kiss her. He barely knew the woman, and he knew it was crazy, but he wanted to kiss her.

A loud call drew their attention. "Your Majesty, we have a tail."

The carriage sped, and Tommy looked out his window to see they were racing for the trees. He looked behind them. Far off in the night were riders racing to catch them.

"The queen's guard," Tommy said angrily. He reached under the seat and pulled out a long, sheathed sword. Alexandra was terrified.

They made it into the woods and halted. The door opened. "Come," Tommy said, offering his hand to Alexandra. They were out of the carriage in moments and hurrying with two of his men deeper into the woods. "They will be after the carriage; we have to get as far away from it as we can," he explained.

Alexandra glanced back to see most of the men were riding to meet the small army who chased them. She was scared for them all.

"You may not know who you are," Tommy said. "But the queen sure does, and you scare her."

"Why me, though? I am just a seamstress," Alexandra argued.

"Please, quiet," one of the guards running with them begged.

They were silent, running with all their might until they found a cave to hide in. Four bodies pressed close to the ground, panting for breath. Far in the distance they heard shouting and the clashing of swords. They stayed still, no one daring to move even an inch.

Alexandra shook, and Tommy took her hand, trying to be reassuring. The fighting went on for a while; all they could do was shiver in the cold, praying for a miracle.

After a while, the man that was keeping watch said, "I can't be certain, but I believe they are retreating."

They remained still until the prince's men returned and called, "We have held them off, but we should move quickly."

Minutes later they were back in the carriage and racing for their lives to Hanton.

Chapter Nineteen

Return to Hanton

"Open for the prince!" the man in Hanton's lookout tower called.

The large gate creaked as it opened slowly. Stomping hoofs came pounding through, the prince's carriage safely between the riders. Without stopping, they hurried until they came to a stop in front of the castle.

Alexandra was looking out her window in amazement at everything. She had seen little of Reigland's riches, but she was certain this kingdom was far more beautiful and wealthier. The walls lined with gold and the pearl-white steps were breathtaking.

"This is yours?" Alexandra breathed out in awe.

"Me and my family," Tommy said. "And many others who live within."

"It is so beautiful," Alexandra said.

"Thank you," Tommy said, though it was her beauty he was staring at.

They were helped out, and Tommy led Alexandra by the arm up the steps. When they entered the front door, a tall gangly man came through the lobby to greet them. "You are back early, Prince Thomas."

The man's face beamed. Alexandra knew she would like him immediately. But when his eyes met hers, he went white as snow. Alexandra thought he would faint.

"Jack?" Tommy asked concerned. "Are you alright?"

Jack tried to snap out of it. "I am sorry," he said. "You just look—you look like someone I knew once, a long time ago."

For a moment Jack thought Christine had walked back into the walls of Hanton. For a mere second in time, he saw his sister coming home. This girl was far too young and more frail than Christine. The likeness was uncanny and he couldn't shake it.

"Jack, this is Lady Alexandra. I confess I near kidnapped her from the Queen of Reigland."

Alexandra blushed. "I am a willing prisoner," she said, curtsying. "It is wonderful to meet you, sir."

Jack shook his head and tried to gather his thoughts. "We thought you would be home late tomorrow."

"We ran into some problems," Tommy told Jack. "We can discuss it in a moment. Where is Tilda?"

"I am here, Your Majesty," the plump woman with greying hair under her cap said as she approached. She looked like she had been pulled abruptly from bed, wrapped snug in a shawl. When she saw Alexandra, she froze, her face going white as Jack's. "Dear Jesus, Mary and Joseph."

Jack nudged her arm and shook his head at her. She tried to regain herself.

"Tilda, this is Lady Alexandra," Tommy said. "Is there a room prepared where she can sleep? She will also need fresh clothes."

"Of course, Your Majesty," Tilda said. "Please, come with me, dear."

Alexandra followed after Tilda, glancing back at Tommy nervously. He gave her a smile and a nod. Alexandra followed Tilda up the stairs, disappearing down a long hall. She was comforted to be taken upstairs and not down to the cellar.

"What was that?" Tommy asked Jack when they were gone. "No, to my room, I must change. Come."

The prince went to his quarters where he was stripped, bathed and then sat in a high- backed chair wrapped in a rich robe, Jack beside him.

"You first," Tommy ordered. "When you saw Alexandra, you'd think she was a ghost."

"She may be," Jack said.

Tommy shook his head. "Tell me."

"I am sorry, Your Majesty," Jack said. "She is the spitting image of my sister who was lost so many years ago. Where did she come from?"

"She was a seamstress to the Queen of Reigland," Tommy explained. "She was raised by the servants. Before I took her with me, she had never even been outside before."

"That is a level of cruelty I do not understand," Jack said. "Are you sure she is not lying to you?"

"Certain," Tommy said. "She had snuck into the ball, which is how I met her. When the queen saw us together, she went into a rage like I've never seen. She wanted to kill the woman. I was able to get her away only because the queen feared the people. When we were out of the city, guards came after us in an effort to kill us. My men fought them off, but I am not certain the efforts are over."

"All over a seamstress?" Jack asked. "Your father will not be happy."

"I know," he said, "but I stand by what I did."

"You better be standing on solid rock," Jack warned. "I will let you rest. We can talk more in the afternoon."

Tommy nodded, and Jack left the room.

Tommy lay in his bed, staring up at the ceiling. Morning was not far off. He thought of Alexandra, her eyes and the way she had danced with him. He did not understand how she had captured his heart so quickly, and he knew he would never be permitted to pursue her, but something about the woman he could not let go.

~

Alexandra woke to the sight of bright rays streaming through her window. She smiled, realizing it hadn't been a dream. Her body sunk deep into the largest, most comfortable bed she had ever seen. Around her were pink walls, golden lamps and white furniture with gold trim. She lay still for a long while, trying to take it in, praying it wouldn't all disappear. Some part of her felt she was dreaming, that she would wake up and all of this would never have happened. But no matter how many times she pinched her arm, the dream remained.

She inhaled deeply, embracing the smell of roses and clean air. She got up from her bed and went to the tall chest, seeking her dress. Then she remembered that Tilda had taken it with her the night before. When she opened the chest, she found beautiful dresses of every color. She slowly ran her fingers across the edges, the fabrics so soft, nothing but beautiful pastels. She picked a light pink dress that flowed freely for movement. Removing her sleeping gown, she dressed herself. Then moving to the small vanity, she found a brush and combed out her silky hair. She looked at herself in the mirror intently and smiled. She was free. She did not know what her life would look like now, but anything would be better than being trapped in that castle, and the prince had promised her she would never be locked up again. She believed him.

An ache pressed her chest as she thought of Bessie and Layla. Perhaps she would see her friend again, but the woman she had only ever known as a mother was gone forever. She knew Bessie would be grateful she had made it out, whisked away by a handsome prince. Deep down, she felt comforted by her spirit.

Standing from the vanity, she walked to the open window and gaped at the sight. Down below was a field of green speckled with flowers of every color, as far as the eye could see. A tear trickled down her cheek. She had heard Layla speak of fields of green grass and fields, but as much as she dreamed, she had never seen one. It was more beautiful than she had imagined. Unlike Raigland, there were no walls holding her in. She could run and keep running, there was nothing to stop her.

She looked beside the window to see the wall was covered with white panels wrapped with vines and speckled with pink, white and red roses. A grin spread across her face as she stepped onto the windowsill, the cold stone smooth against her bare feet, and reached to grab the wooden gate to climb down it. Thankfully, it supported her weight, and she descended slowly until her foot hit damp dirt and green grass. She stood still, her heart beating fast, trying to wake herself to her reality. She was standing on the other side of the wall, feet planted in grass and dirt. It felt like a dream and she would float away with the wind.

She turned and looked at the endless field before her, a yellow sun shining down. Alexandra drew in a deep breath, picked up her skirt and began to run. She ran as fast as she could, not in fear, but in freedom. She ran like a bird who has just found its wings. Her hair and skirt flew just like her heart. She threw her arms to the sky and spun around, laughing at herself with joy. When she stopped to catch her breath, she noticed the prince a little way off, sitting on top of a hill on his horse. The horse was snow white, and Alexandra thought he was magnificent. The prince smiled at her and rode her way. She stood still and waited.

Part of her was frightened he would scold her for running out, perhaps lock her away. But the look in his eyes reassured her as he came to a stop.

"Good morning, sweet lady," Tommy said. "You look like you rested well."

"Your Majesty, I cannot thank you enough—"

"Think nothing of it," Tommy said. "A woman like you does not belong in a place like that."

Alexandra blushed. "Thank you."

"Have you ridden?" he asked, patting the side of his horse's neck.

"No," she said.

"Ride with me," he said, dismounting and reaching out his hand.

The horse was tall, and it made Alexandra nervous. But after a life hidden away, she wouldn't shy away now. "Alright." She accepted his hand timidly.

"This is Duke," Tommy told her. "He is my horse."

"He is beautiful," Alexandra said. Looking up at Duke's long face, Alexandra wondered how she would ever get on him.

"Here," Tommy said, helping her onto the horse. He hopped on behind her and took the reins. "Trust me," was the last thing he said. Then they were off.

The air left Alexandra's chest. She gripped the horse's mane, Tommy's arms wrapped snug around her so she wouldn't fall. Duke ran across the green grass, the two of them jolting up and down with every stride. Alexandra's smile was uncontainable. Her body shook with thrill, giving way fear and filling with bliss. Throwing out her arms, she embraced the breeze and golden sun on her skin. Tommy smiled behind her, his heart swelling within him.

After riding a while, they returned to the front of the castle. "I hope you don't mind; I find the door a little easier," Tommy teased.

She blushed, realizing he must have seen her descend the wall.

When they were inside, Tilda ran up in a frenzy. "Good Lord, child, you had me terrified. Where have you been?"

"I am sorry, I just went for a run," Alexandra explained. "It was so beautiful outside, I admit I climbed down the wall."

"Climbed down the—well, my goodness." Tilda clenched her heart.

Tommy chuckled. "Go get washed up. Will you join me for lunch later?"

"I would be honored," Alexandra said, willingly following Tilda.

"Prince Thomas," Jack said, walking up, "your father is requesting an audience in his office."

Tommy sighed. "I cannot hide forever, can I?"

"I am afraid he is insistent," Jack said apologetically.

Tommy nodded and followed Jack to his father's office.

Prince Thomas was sitting at his desk, quill in hand, writing. There was a knock at his door. "Enter," he said.

Jack opened the door, and Tommy walked in behind. Thomas turned his eyes upward without moving his head. "Leave us, Jack," he said.

Jack bowed and returned through the door he had come in, closing it behind him.

Tommy stood still, waiting for his father to acknowledge him. Thomas did not hurry, finishing what he was doing, setting the quill in ink and finally rising to his feet, meeting his son with a deadly stare. "What the hell were you thinking?"

"Sir, I assure you—"

"Do you not understand the fragile alliance between us and that dreaded woman?" Thomas asked. He was angry. "You would risk our entire kingdom over one girl?"

"She was going to kill her," Tommy said boldly.

"Do you even know who this woman is?" Thomas demanded.

"Alexandra," Tommy said simply. "She was the queen's seamstress."

Thomas stared coldly at his son, his thoughts very clear.

"A seamst—you do not know who she is," Thomas said. "For all you know, she could be in cahoots with her queen to have you or I or even the king murdered!"

"She would not do that," Tommy argued. "Yes, I have only known Alexandra for a short time, but I am certain. She is not dangerous. She is just a girl who has been given no freedom or chance for a real life, with no reason why. I stand by my choice."

"And the consequences that come with it?" Thomas asked, banging a hand on his desk. "You were attacked; two of your men were wounded. Over one girl!"

"And does that not seem odd to you?" Tommy pressed. "You are right; I do not know the whole story. Perhaps that is foolish, but clearly there is something about her that scares Queen Cora."

Thomas gave an exasperated sigh and fell back into his chair. He sat and thought for a few moments. "We will have men keep watch for any future attacks from Reigland. For now, she can stay, but all of my men will be instructed to keep a hawk's eye on every move she makes."

"Thank you, Father," Tommy said.

"One more thing," Thomas said, meeting Tommy's eyes with a warning glare. "Do not fall for this girl. I heard about your little ride this morning."

"News does travel fast."

"No matter what story lies behind her, she is a commoner, and you will marry nothing less than a princess. Do I make myself clear?"

Tommy nodded, accepting his father's words.

"Leave me now," Thomas said. "There is much to do, and thanks to you, there is now even more. I am trying to find a way to mend the breach you've caused between Reigland and us."

Without another word, Tommy obeyed his father and left.

Tommy sought out Jack immediately and pulled him aside. "I know my father fears Alexandra's presence here, but I believe it is in vain. Please, make sure she is safe no matter what happens."

"You know my loyalty is to your father first," Jack said. "However, I agree with you that there is something about this woman. I will keep her in my sight."

"I thank you," Tommy said, placing a hand on Jack's shoulder. "Damn my father's demands I only court royals."

"She is a beautiful woman," Jack agreed. "But you and I both know there is no way around a law."

"Her eyes," Tommy continued. "I cannot explain it. When she looks at me, I swear I am her captive. Have there ever seen eyes so sharp and blue?"

"I have seen eyes like that before," Jack said. "A long time ago; my sister."

"Do you think she could be related to you?" Tommy asked.

"No," Jack said. "She was the only one left in her family. There were no others."

"Only one?" Tommy asked. "She was your sister."

"My parents adopted her—it is a long story," Jack dismissed.

Sensing Jack did not want to confide further, Tommy moved on. "She will remain here, at least until and if she finds another place to go. I want her to have a better life. A woman like that deserves so much more. She should be draped in riches and cared for eternally."

"My dear prince, if you let her go, she has a chance to find love with another man worthy of her. Perhaps a duke," Jack said.

Tommy felt a pang of jealousy, which he tried to fight. "We will see what the future holds."

Over the next few months, Alexandra settled into her new home at the castle. No matter how hard she tried, no one would let her work. They just looked after her and draped her with beautiful clothes and jewels and fed her rich foods. Alexandra finally talked the gardener into letting her help with the flowers. She loved having her hands in the dirt and watching the flowers grow and bloom. She basked in the warm sun and worked tirelessly.

She also talked Tilda into letting her help the seamstress. Everyone was impressed at how skilled and fast she was. She made dresses so beautiful that the queen herself wore them.

Prince Thomas refused to meet her, angry with his son for the complications and dangers her presence had caused. There were no further threats from Reigland, and for that, everyone was grateful.

And despite the warning to not fall for a common woman, Tommy could not resist sneaking away to ride with Alexandra and have picnics beneath the blue sky. His father knew, of course, but he decided to not fight it unless Tommy tried to pursue the girl romantically.

No matter what anyone said or did, Prince Thomas II was falling hard for the mysterious and beautiful Alexandra. And though his father ruled his actions, he could not stop his heart.

Chapter Twenty

The Spring Ball

It was time for Hanton's Spring Ball, the time when the kingdom gathered to celebrate the season. It was a beautiful time, always filled with flowers, music, and delicious foods. Alexandra sewed beautiful dresses for the queen and princesses and was even able to help the gardener arrange fresh flowers all over the vast, golden ballroom. Her life was full and happy in Hanton, and though the feelings between her and the prince were guarded, she loved her life.

The Spring Ball was Prince Thomas's least favorite time of year. Almost no one understood why, but his feelings were unchanging. His wife would always coax him into going, but his agreement did not diminish how much he despised it.

"Not this year, Diana," Thomas pleaded with his wife as she examined herself in the mirror. He was sitting on the edge of their bed in black trousers, his white shirt hung open.

"Do you like this dress?" Diana asked, ignoring her husband's plea. "That Alexandra girl made it. She is incredible."

"So our son has said," Thomas gritted. "Diana, please."

"The Spring Ball is one of the most important events of the entire year," Diana explained. "The Royal Family is expected to be there. Everyone is expected to be there. Honestly, husband, I do not understand why you hate it so.”

“But you know that I do,” Thomas continued. “So why do you press me? Every damn year.”

Diana sat next to Thomas and took his face in her hands. “My dear prince, I know how you carried every worry of the world on your shoulders. But this is important. What can I do to help make it easier?”

Thomas let his head fall into her shoulder and she stroked his hair lovingly. “Not this time,” he said.

Of course, Diana eventually coaxed Thomas around. He made it clear he would only attend for an hour and was not going to be happy. It was hard for Diana, she loved Thomas but she knew something had always kept him from giving his heart to her. In his own way she knew he loved her too, but something held him back. A worry like stones hung around his neck.

Alexandra was giddy in expectation of the night’s ball. She had snuck into her last ball and nearly been killed. This time she was going by invitation from a prince, and she could not wait.

She was fitted into her dress; her hair was done up with fresh flowers. Even she had to admit she looked ravishing. She wondered if she would meet a man this evening who could take her mind off the handsome prince who seemed to own her every thought.

Her heart soared as she entered the beautiful ballroom and was introduced as a lady. She sipped on fine wine, laughed with newfound friends and swayed to the music from the orchestra. How different than the last time! She was a little embarrassed at the way she kept to the edges of the room, hugging the walls. She wasn't afraid of the crowd, but Prince Thomas, his princess and the king and queen all sat at the far end of the room surveying the ball. She knew how much Prince Thomas did not approve of her presence, refusing to meet her, and the thought of his stern stare falling upon her was frightening. She knew he wouldn't strike off her head, but she would be much happier if she never had to meet royalty again. Except, of course, for Tommy.

But she couldn't help stealing glances, seeing the white-haired king whisper into his queen's ear, causing her to giggle. She relaxed at the sight, so different from the king and queen of Reigland. A couple of gentlemen tried to ask Alexandra to dance, but as much as she tried to be brave, she turned them down, not ready to draw attention.

"Some party," she heard a familiar voice behind her.

Alexandra smiled and turned, looking up to see the handsome prince standing over her.

"It is, isn't it?" Alexandra replied.

"You look exquisite," Tommy admired.

"And you are devilish," Alexandra giggled.

A dangerous sparkle shot through Tommy's eye. "A charge I cannot deny," he said, then bowed and offered his hand. "Dance with me."

"What if your father sees?" Alexandra asked anxiously as Tommy pulled her to the floor.

"It is a ball, what is he going to do?" Tommy asked, brushing off her worries.

"Someone wanted to kill me last time we danced," Alexandra reminded him.

"Not here."

As they moved onto the floor, Alexandra saw everyone else had vanished, leaving Prince Thomas II and Lady Alexandra as the only two people in the middle of the room, every single eye on them.

"The last time we did this it ended very badly," Alexandra whispered when Tommy pulled her into him. Their hearts pounded against each other.

"Trust me," he said with a wink.

The music struck, and Tommy began to move, Alexandra following with perfect grace within his strong arms. Seeing them, Prince Thomas grew red and gritted his teeth. "What the bloody hell is he doing?"

Diana put a hand on his. "Please, husband," she said. "Remain calm. He is just dancing with her."

The entire room was captured by the way she moved. She was breathtaking, spinning all around the dance floor with the prince. They soared together. Tommy lifted her hand above her head, and she spun, around and around again, her skirt flying revealing the rose on her ankle. From his seat, Thomas's eyes grew wide and his heart beat like thunder, entire body shaking.

"Thomas," Diana asked in worry at the pale, wide-eyed look on her husband's face.

Then she jumped in surprise as Thomas began to laugh. His face bright, eyes on the two dancing, he laughed loudly. He laughed until he was crying, tears streaming down both sides of his face. He covered his mouth in surprise and shook his head.

"Good heavens, what has gotten into you?" Diana asked, unable to keep from laughing as well, completely unsure of what was so funny and amazed to see joy on her husband's face. It was something she had never seen before, even at their wedding and the birth of their five children. But here he was, not just smiling, but laughing. Laughing like a man who has just found freedom.

He pulled his eyes away from the two dancing and looked at his princess sitting beside him. Taking her hand firmly, he said, "Thank you for being such a stubborn woman."

"You're welcome?" she said, unsure. And to her surprise, he kissed her, just because he wanted to.

When he released her, she said, "Well, I still do not know what is wrong with you, but I like it."

They looked back at the floor where Tommy spun Alexandra around and then stopped in a dramatic pose as the last note faded. The room erupted in claps and cheers from every direction. Face to face and eye to eye, the prince could not hold himself back anymore, and he kissed Alexandra. Without hesitation, Alexandra kissed him back.

When they turned to look at the cheering crowd, Tommy was surprised to see his father, on his feet, clapping for them. A smile he had never in his life seen was plastered on his face. He looked at his mother, who shrugged that she had no idea what happened.

"Come," Tommy said, taking Alexandra's hand and leading her to where the king, queen, and his parents all were. "Father, this is Alexandra."

Thomas stepped down to the floor and wrapped Alexandra in an embrace. "It is my greatest honor to meet you."

His smile then fell as quickly as it had come. "Your mother," he asked, "where is she?"

"I never knew my parents," Alexandra said. "I believe they both died when I was a baby."

Thomas's face contorted. Then through tears, he said, "If you will excuse me."

Luke and Tara watched Thomas leave, unsure what had just happened. Diana went after him. Tommy looked at Alexandra. "I've never seen my father smile before," he said.

~

Diana followed Thomas down the hall. Jack was close behind them. "Thomas," Diana called.

Thomas finally stopped and turned, his face wet with tears. "I want to laugh with the greatest joy, yet I want to weep with even greater loss."

"Darling," Diana hugged him tenderly, "tell me what is going on, please."

Jack came up behind, his face just as distorted. Thomas looked up from his wife's shoulder. "Tell me I am not crazy," he pleaded with Jack. "Tell me you saw it too."

"It was pretty unmistakable," Jack agreed.

"Saw what? I swear, if one of you men do not tell me what is going on!" Diana was frustrated and concerned.

"When that girl was dancing," Jack began to explain. "Alexandra. Did you notice anything about her ankle?"

"How could I notice anything with my husband losing his mind beside me?" Diana asked with exasperation.

"On her ankle, there was a birthmark," Jack continued. "A distinct rose."

"The only people who have ever been born with that mark were the royals of Dancé," Thomas finished.

"Dancé?" Diana asked, "You mean that kingdom that was destroyed decades ago? I honestly thought it was a legend."

"It is not," Jack said. "I was conceived there. When Dancé was destroyed, my parents sought solace here in Hanton. We were not alone though; the princess—rather, the rightful queen—who was about six weeks old at that time was with us. We were going to tell her who she was when she was eighteen, but days before, she ran away, never to be found.”

“I spent eighteen years with my men rebuilding that kingdom,” Thomas said, a far-off look in his eye. “Only to have its queen disappear right before we returned her home. We could never find her, and she never returned.”

“My father spent about two years searching,” Jack said. “Nothing.”

“Well Alexandra is very young,” Diana said. “She could not be—”

“The only explanation,” Thomas cut in, “is that Alexandra must be Christine’s daughter.”

“You mean to say, that girl is a queen?” Diana asked. “And we have her sewing dresses and working the garden?”

“Yes,” Thomas confessed.

“That explains why she was hidden away,” Jack said, more recognition in his eyes. “The last place my father went was to Reigland. He spoke to the queen and was told they had not seen Christine. My father always said he had a bad feeling about that woman. If she put together that Christine was a queen, perhaps—” he could not finish the thought, but they all knew.

“What a horrid woman!” Diana said.

“I suppose the question is, what do we do now?” Jack asked.

Thomas did not have to wonder. "We take her to Dancé. We explain everything and finally return a queen to the throne."

"Tommy will want to go with her," Diana said.

"Thomas," Thomas corrected. "And if he wants to wed himself to a queen, he had better adopt his given name. King Tommy is ludicrous."

Diana giggled quietly at her husband.

"Let them enjoy tonight," Thomas said. "And let us all rest and come to terms with this. Tomorrow I will speak to my father and we can prepare to escort her home."

Jack nodded. "As you command."

In the ballroom, the night continued with laughter, freedom, and dance. Thomas took his wife to bed and loved her like he had never loved her before, finally freed from the demons that had haunted him for so many years. And Jack went to see his father.

Sir David had been sick and near death's door for months. It was hard for Jack to visit him, the frail sight of his body too heartbreaking. But when he left Thomas and Diana, Jack knew he had to tell his father.

Jack entered the room to see his father lying in his bed, eyes closed. Jack went and sat next to him quietly, thinking him asleep.

"I am neither asleep nor dead," David said unmoved.

Jack smiled at his father. "I would think nothing less."

Jack turned up the lamp beside David's bed. Opening his weak eyes, David used every effort to sit up. Jack helped him, propping pillows behind him.

"To what do I owe the pleasure of my son's visit on the night of a ball?" David asked.

Jack sat quietly for a minute, looking at his hands. He did not know where to begin.

"Father, I believe we were right in assuming Christine was gone," Jack said.

"Was there news?" David asked anxiously.

"A girl, orphan, who could not be anything but Christine's daughter has found refuge here," Jack explained.

"You are certain?"

"She has the birthmark."

David gasped, tears welling in his eyes. "If Christine is lost, at least when I die and meet her at the gates of heaven, I can tell her that her daughter will inherit her throne. Dancé will no longer be without a queen."

Jack's eyes welled. "Your duty to Michael and Anna is fulfilled."

"Thank you," David said quietly, closing his eyes. "Take good care of that girl."

"I promise."

Jack did not leave his father's side all night, his hand grasping his. Early in the morning, before the sun rose, David's hand slipped from Jack's grasp, and his heart quit beating. Jack wept over his father, hugging his lifeless body. Now he was as alone in the world as Alexandra. There was nothing left for him but the mission from his father to protect Alexandra and get her safely home.

When Thomas and Luke were informed of David's passing, they hurried to Jack, who would not leave his father's side.

"We can wait," Luke said. "Bury your father and then take Alexandra home in a few days."

"No," Jack said. "Waiting to mourn is what made us lose Christine. And I know my father would want to be laid to rest in Dancé."

Luke nodded, "I believe you are right. We will all go. David meant so much to all of us, and after all this, we should be there to return the queen to her throne."

"I am with Jack as well," Thomas said. "David should be buried in Dancé."

"When the sun has risen, we will prepare," Luke commanded.

Both men agreed, and David's body was readied for his trip home.

Chapter Twenty-One

The Queen Comes Home

The next morning, Tommy went into his father's office. Thomas had sent for his son at first light. Tommy was walking like a puppy who knew he would be scolded by his master. Despite the momentary joy, Tommy knew his father would not be happy about that kiss. He knocked on Thomas's door.

"Come in," Thomas welcomed.

Tommy opened the door slowly and walked in with his head bowed. Thomas glanced up and then rose to his feet. "My son, thank you for meeting me."

Tommy looked at his father. "I know you are not happy with my actions—"

Thomas lifted a firm hand to silence him. "Let me decide how I feel about your actions. Please sit." Not understanding, Tommy moved to sit across from Thomas. "Under any other circumstances, I probably would have sent Alexandra packing and dealt with you harshly."

"But?"

"It came to our attention last night that your Lady Alexandra is someone we have been looking for, for a very long time," Thomas explained.

"I do not understand."

"Do you remember the tales I told you about Dancé when you were a boy?"

"The kingdom burned," Tommy said, "leaving behind a lost queen with no home. In every version, she never found her way there."

"It was not a story," Thomas said. "It was real. I spent most of my life before marrying your mother working to rebuild Dancé, and the last remaining heir was kept safe in our walls. Until she ran. We did not get the chance to tell her the truth. We have had every reason to believe her dead, and we still believe that. But not without leaving behind a child."

"Alexandra?" Tommy asked in disbelief.

Thomas nodded, "Your lady is not a lady, she is actually a queen with a kingdom waiting for her."

"Cora—she must have known," Tommy said.

"We have reason to believe she did," Thomas replied. "We are certain of little, however, this is what we are left with."

"So, what does this mean?" Tommy asked.

"It means we will be taking Alexandra home today," Thomas said. "And after all these years, Dancé will have its queen. It will flourish and once again be more than just a legend."

"Well, I am going too," Tommy said.

"I assumed as much," Thomas smirked. "Which is why I called you in here. I understand that despite my previous distaste, you have been courting Alexandra. Am I right to assume you want more from the relationship?"

"If you are asking if I want to marry Alexandra, the answer is most certainly yes."

Thomas nodded. "As Alexandra is queen, you would be devoted to Dancé, and if she accepts you, would rule by her side as king. The relationship between Hanton and Dancé has always been that of brotherhood. Still, your home would be there, and your loyalty with it."

"I love you, Father, and love my country," Tommy said. "But if the choice is there, I choose Alexandra and whatever comes with her."

"Do not say anything to her," Thomas said. "We ride to Dancé today. All will be explained to her there."

"Yes, sir." Tommy rose to his feet and Thomas with him.

"Oh, and one more thing," Thomas said. "If you wish to marry and inherit the role of king, it is time to inherit your given name. 'Tommy' is not the name of a king."

Thomas II bowed to his father in acceptance and turned to leave.

~

Thomas's heart was pounding louder than it ever had. Before him was the most beautiful kingdom, propped up beside a cascading ocean. Stone and glass he had laid with his own hands. Thomas had realized years ago that he would never get to bring Christine here, never place a crown on her head and give her the throne. But while his heart mourned for Christine, he was overwhelmed with the anticipation of returning the legacy home. Anxiety mingled with excitement; his hands that gripped the reins shook. He wanted to laugh and thought he would cry, both of which he had done in excess since the night before.

Dancé had been settled by a growing number of people over the years. His men who had worked so faithfully to help build wanted to stay, the place having become home and many farmers as well. They and their families had taken residence, the kingdom ruled by Hanton as its daughter.

Thomas was leading the caravan. When they reached the city gate, a crowd had gathered, expecting them. Seeing William, one of Thomas's lead men, he smiled broadly and dismounted, walking to embrace the man.

"I could not believe it when we received your message," William said. "Is it true? Our queen's daughter come to claim her throne?"

"It is, my friend," Thomas said. "Though we have not told her yet."

"No better way than to show her, eh?"

"Exactly."

"Come, bring everyone. We have prepared food, and the throne room has been readied," William said, his feet in motion.

"You waste no time, my friend," Thomas smiled.

Alexandra was in a carriage near the back of the group with Tilda, who had been beaming ridiculously all morning. Alexandra had asked if she had started drinking early, to which Tilda just laughed and shook her head.

Alexandra leaned her head out the window and looked in amazement upon the kingdom before her. White stone walls and a flag of deep purple with a golden crest, a rose wrapped in vine that seemed to dance. Alexandra's ears perked at the sound of waves crashing against an ocean. "What is this place?" she asked Tilda, not looking away from the sights. Far ahead she saw Thomas speaking with another man she did not recognize. When they moved forward, the small crowd followed.

"A place of legends," Tilda said.

"I hear the ocean," Alexandra told her.

"Yes," Tilda confirmed. "We will have to take a walk on the beach later."

Alexandra waited anxiously, her head hanging from the window trying to see. Tilda held in a laugh. When their carriage finally reached the castle gate, Thomas II came to open the door. Extending his hand, he helped Alexandra down.

"Thank you, Majesty," she said sweetly.

There seemed to be an almost mischievous glimmer in his eye that she had never seen before, but it made her feel a little giddy. Taking his offered arm, they followed the group making their way inside.

Alexandra could not stop looking at everything. Her eyes wandered along the walls hung with paintings and rich tapestries, the ceiling holding sparkling chandeliers. Everyone in the castle was working quickly to prepare for a party, it seemed, and as they passed by, she noticed them looking and smiling at her.

"They don't get many visitors, do they?" Alexandra asked Thomas II.

"They will soon," he winked.

"What do you mean?"

Before he could answer her, two large doors were opened, and they entered the most beautiful ballroom Alexandra had ever seen. Tall pillars were draped in purple cloth. A balcony surrounded the entire room, and the walls were painted with people dancing through clouds. A feast was prepared, and a band sat to play. Two thrones sat golden and high at the far end of the room, but Alexandra noted that they were empty. In fact, aside from the servants preparing, there was no one else there but them. Alexandra did not dare ask any questions, surrounded by so many of high rank.

Thomas moved into the middle of the room, turned to look at everyone with a massive smile, clapped his hands together and said, "I am so thankful to have each one of you here today. Welcome to the reborn kingdom of Dancé."

Everyone cheered and clapped. Alexandra was still unsure what was going on, so she just went along.

"Most of us here had some hand in bringing this together," Thomas continued. "My men and I spent years building Dancé back up the ruins."

"Your father helped build this place?" Alexandra whispered to Thomas II.

"Yes," he confirmed. "It was burned to the ground years ago. My father helped bring it back to its original glory."

"Too many years we have prayed for this day," Thomas continued. "And like me, I am sure most of you thought it would never come. Alexandra, would you accompany me?"

Alexandra looked at Thomas II questioningly, but he gave her a reassuring nod and nudge. Alexandra walked to Thomas's offered hand and let him lead her to the far end of the room. Everyone else following behind.

Where Thomas led, Alexandra noticed something built into the wall, glass with a flower sealed inside.

"This flower," Thomas explained to Alexandra, "was worn by the last royal to ever live here, Queen Christine, though she never had the chance to claim her throne. She was strong-willed and independent. This flower fell from her hair during a dance when she was young. I had it sealed so that for the rest of eternity, a piece of her would always be represented." Thomas ran a gentle finger down the side of the glass and then looked at Alexandra. "She was your mother."

Alexandra looked at Thomas as if she hadn't heard him right. Surely, she hadn't. "I don't understand."

"Everyone of royal blood born to Dancé had two things that distinguished them," Thomas explained. "One was a ridiculous natural ability to dance unlike any other, and the second was a birthmark, always found on the ankle, shaped like a rose."

Alexandra's brow crinkled. She thought of the first time Thomas II had asked her to dance, how frightened she had been, only to soar as if she'd been doing it all her life. And, of course, the mark; there was no question that sounded like her ankle.

"There must be some mistake," Alexandra tried to reason.

"There is no mistake, dear," Tara said coming to the other side of her. "You are the spitting image of your mother. I should have seen it sooner."

"But my parents were—" she stopped, remembering she did not know who her parents were. "Then how did I end up in Reigland? In the service of Queen Cora?"

"We do not know all the details," Thomas admitted. "Your mother was living in Hanton while we were rebuilding. She was just a baby when Dancé was destroyed. At eighteen, she ran away. The details following are unknown. We never found her."

"Then how are you certain this woman was my mother?" Alexandra asked. She wanted to cry. Her whole life had been an imprisoned confusion, and now she was being told she was royalty?

"You bear her mark," Thomas said gently, "that is no accident."

Alexandra lifted her skirt and looked down at her ankle, the pink rose clear and unmistakable.

"I—may I have a minute?" Alexandra asked.

"Of course," Tara said gently.

Thomas offered his arm. "There is a garden; I will take you there. I have been told how you love the flowers."

"Yes, Your Majesty," Alexandra said, accepting his arm and following him through the back, out to the garden.

Alexandra's skin was white as snow, her fingers tingling and palms damp. Her head seemed to swim with the chaos in her mind. She heard what was said, but it seemed to bounce off her like water off a rock. She couldn't even take in the glory around her. The birds that sang happily were drowned out by her thumping heart.

Thomas led Alexandra to a bench and had her sit down. Before her were three swings hanging from a tree. Something about them drew her attention. She stared for a while, thinking of the family she was deprived of. No matter who they were, servants nor kings, either way, they had been taken from her. Somehow not knowing seemed easier than knowing. Tears began to fall down her face.

Thomas was sitting next to her silently, allowing her to process everything.

"You said this place—Dancé—it was rebuilt?" Alexandra asked after a few minutes of silence.

"Yes," Thomas confirmed. "When your mother was only weeks old, there was a celebration ball for her. During the celebration, Dancé was attacked. Almost everyone was murdered, and everything burned straight to the ground. Sir David and his wife were the only ones who made it out. They rescued your mother. They sought refuge in Hanton, which is how we were so closely connected to your mother and the rebuilding."

"My whole life," Alexandra said, "I have not known who I am or where I came from. There is a relief in knowing, but it comes with a heavy sadness. I guess some part of me thought one day my parents would show up, that they were out there looking for me. I have always wanted a family, more than anything."

"You have one," Thomas said taking her hands. "No, we are not your parents or your brothers, but we loved your mother like she was our own, and we will love you the same."

Alexandra finally met Thomas's eyes and gave him a weak smile. "Thank you."

Thomas nodded, "It is also no secret that my son has more than a fancy for you."

Alexandra laughed a little and wiped a tear from her face. "This will take a while to sink in."

"Of course," Thomas agreed. "And we will all be here for you as you do so. Alexandra, we may be giving you a home and the truth, but what you are giving us is so much more. Decades of heartache and uncertainty are brought to a blessed end by your presence."

Alexandra took a deep breath. "So what now?"

"Once you are ready, you will be crowned Queen," Thomas said gleefully. "We will not abandon you; we will support you in any way we can until you are ready to take it all on your own. This place has been filling with men and woman eager to protect and serve in your castle and live in your kingdom."

"It is impossible," Alexandra breathed, looking out at the glorious garden.

"All things are possible."

~

David was laid to rest behind the castle, beside the pillars left for Michael and Anna. Word spread quickly through all the land, the most incredible news of redemption, a miracle no one could believe. A queen was being crowned, the legend returning to life. Thousands traveled for days, weeks to see if what they heard was true.

Alexandra tried to let it sink in. Life now felt like a dream. She was showered in riches and gowns, trained in royal etiquette, taught the history of her kingdom. She felt overwhelmed by her responsibilities. Tilda chose to stay in Dancé, taking charge of Alexandra's daily care. Stephen also accepted the role of captain of the guard. Thomas and Diana spent most of their time in Dancé, personally helping and training Alexandra. Thomas II was never out of sight.

Word was sent discreetly and Layla and her father were brought to live in Dancé. Alexandra missed Bessie, the only mother she had ever known, but to have her lifelong friend back safely in her new life was more than a blessing.

The day of Alexandra's coronation, Dancé was back to life as never before. A ball grander than anything anyone had seen, the walls bursting with people wanting to lay eyes on the new queen.

When Alexandra entered the room, all hearts stopped. She was the image of the queens who had reigned before her—grandmother, great-grandmother—gloriously beautiful, with hair that shone like the sun and eyes that sparkled like the sea. She was adorned in purple silk and wreathed in pearls, head held high. Music played triumphantly as Alexandra floated with grace to kneel before the throne where Thomas waited with a face that shone brighter than day.

Alexandra knelt before him, and Thomas took the golden crown studded with diamonds and rubies, which sat on a velvet pillow.

Thomas lifted the crown in the air and placed it down on her head, proclaiming her Queen. The crown felt heavy and awkward, but Alexandra felt like an angel. She rose, allowing Thomas to lead her to the high throne where she sat. The moment she did, the entire room erupted in cheers of praise. Nothing like it had ever been heard or seen before.

"Long live the Queen!" Thomas called.

"Long live the Queen!" echoed through the entire castle.

Stepping down and leaving Alexandra on her throne, crowned and home, peace finally settled on Thomas. Diana met him, and he embraced her, tears of relief and joy falling from his face.

Jack who had found his home in Dancé was mingling and dancing with a swarm of friends. A joy in him he had not known since childhood.

When the party was in full swing, Thomas II went to stand before Alexandra's throne and bowed, "May I be so bold as to ask Her Majesty the Queen for the honor of a dance?"

"It did take you long enough," Alexandra beamed.

Alexandra accepted his hand and followed him to the middle of the floor. What followed was elegance, grace, purity, and love. The feeling in every breathe was indescribable. Everything broken suddenly felt mended, every heart made whole.

When they were finished dancing, Thomas II whispered into her ear, "I want to show you something."

Taking her hand, they escaped through a back door.

They heard the sound of strong waves crashing on the shore and the night breeze blowing. Hand in hand, shoes abandoned, Thomas II and Alexandra stepped out onto the sand. Alexandra picked up her coronation dress to prance beside him, the two of them laughing and free, cold water racing to their feet. From the tower above, Stephen watched protectively, smiling at the joy before him.

Breathless, Thomas stopped and pulled Alexandra into him. She gazed up into his eyes, luxuriating in the feeling of warmth and safety within his arms. The way he looked, she thought he would kiss her. She was dying for him to kiss her. Over the last few weeks he was always there, but with a certain distance, as if waiting for the moment, but making sure he was never forgotten.

"I love you," he said, sure and bold. "You are my first thought when I wake and the last before I sleep. The reason for so my smiles and the joy behind my laughter. I may not be fool enough to believe in love at first sight, but that doesn't change the truth. You swept me away the first time we danced. And you've been taking a firmer hold of my heart with every passing day."

Alexandra could feel his body shaking against hers. "Thomas—"

"Please," he said, "let me get through this."

Releasing her body, he took her hand. His skin was wet and cold against her warmth. Then he moved down to his knee, his eyes never leaving hers. His knee sunk into the sand. An ambitious wave lapped against his thigh, but he barely noticed.

"Oh," she breathed.

"Alexandra," he said, "would you accept my hand? Just a lowly prince who wants to love you eternally."

"You saved my life," Alexandra said. "You saw me as valuable when I was nothing. You loved me when it was forbidden. And do you think a crown on my head would change a thing?"

Alexandra sank to her knees next to him, forgetting her dress in the water. "I love you," she told him.

Thomas breathed out a laugh of relief and pure happiness. Reaching in his pocket, he revealed a ring with the largest diamond Alexandra had ever seen. "Oh my Lord!"

"Do you like it?" Thomas asked.

"Oh, just put it on and kiss me, fool," Alexandra said, her eyes glistening with tears.

Thomas laughed and slipped the golden band on her finger. Then he looked up at her; combing his fingers in the back of her hair, he pulled her body into his and kissed her. He kissed her with a greater passion than any man before him. In the sand swept by waves, beneath the glow of her kingdom, finally, everything was whole.

Epilogue

After their marriage, King Thomas and Queen Alexandra had two unexpected visitors brought before their throne.

"Your Majesty," the man said, "we are so happy to meet you. My name is Henry; this is my wife Isabell."

"Welcome," Alexandra said. "I was told you knew something about my parents."

"Yes," Henry said quickly. "Do forgive me, we have been traveling, and we never thought—"

Isabell grabbed Henry's hand. "We were friends with your parents, very close friends. There the day they met, wed and—when you were born."

"Where are they?" Alexandra asked anxiously.

"Cora," Henry explained. "She had them murdered the day you were born."

"She killed them and then burned down their home," Isabell continued, "in an effort to make it look like an accident. We thought you were killed in the fire. Oh, sweet girl, if we had known—" Isabell choked. "I am so sorry."

Alexandra looked at her husband. Thomas said to them, "How do we know that what you are saying is true?"

"Here." Henry revealed two paintings covered in cloth. Lifting the cloth, they saw a painting of a young woman who looked just like

Alexandra. She was sitting in a field of tall grass, a hat clutched in her hand, skirt lifted enough to see the rose on her ankle. "Matthew, your father, loved to paint. He did this of your mother."

Tears welled in Alexandra's eyes. Cora had taken so much from her; it seemed every day she learned of more that was stolen. Seeing the image of her mother, gazing off into the distance, hair wild and free, a smile so gentle; it made Alexandra's heart ache.

"My father?" she asked.

Henry moved that painting to reveal a second. This one was of the same woman, a man standing behind her, holding her in his arms. Pure light shone from both their faces.

"Your father was the captain of the king's guard. After the king's passing, Matthew was assigned to Queen Cora."

"They were happy," Alexandra noted quietly.

"Oh yes," Isabell agreed, "the happiest people you've ever seen. And so in love."

"Why—" Alexandra choked, her welling eyes staring at the images of her parents. "Why would Cora do this?"

"Cora was spoiled with goods but deprived of love," Isabell explained, "and she had her eye set on Matthew since they were young. But Matthew grew to be a man, and Cora wanted to keep playing children's games."

"She was very angry when he married Christine—your mother," Henry said. "No one is certain what made her finally break, but the rumor was that a man came to visit and told Cora that Christine was of royal blood.”

“It sent her over,” Isabell finished.

“My dear girl, if we had known—” Henry started.

“No,” Alexandra injected. “I only met Cora a couple of times, but that was enough to see who she was. She tried to have me killed merely for leaving with my king.” She touched Thomas’s hand, and he smiled at her.

“I will send word to King Alabe,” Thomas said. “Cora should be held responsible for her actions.”

Alexandra rose and walked down to meet Henry and Isabell. “You are welcome to stay here, though I have one request of you.”

“Anything, child,” Isabell said.

“Tell me about my parents,” Alexandra asked. “Tell me everything.”

And so Henry and Isabell made Dancé their home. They set up a new clinic and were loved and cherished. King Thomas sent word to King Alabe and the Reigland nobility of Cora’s betrayal and murder of a king and queen. Alabe dithered, still afraid of his queen, but the Reigland nobility and army decided they had had enough; Hanton was far too dangerous a foe. Cora was beheaded for her crimes. Alabe married another who bore him many sons, and Reigland prospered under his rule.

Thomas and Alexandra had many sons and daughters. Each seemed to dance from her womb and bore the mark of Dancé. For generations they have lived on, ruling with kindness and love, spreading hope and magic to all they meet.

Now this tale of Christine and her daughter has ended. But the legend of Dancé lives on. Spreading its magic, carrying on kindness and love forever.

So I leave you with this question; legend or legendary? Open your eyes and see. Some say to this day they have sighted an unusual mark and ability to move beyond anything you can imagine. Living among us and we would never know, spreading magic through their dance.

If you dare to believe.

The End

Special Thanks

It took over 13 years from the birth of this story for it to reach publication. I cannot explain the thrill of the little teenage girl inside me knowing that her book is finally reaching the world.

I could not close the last page without acknowledging just a couple of people who have supported me through this recent journey of publication.

My husband Brent, for loving me through it all. Jessica, Heather, Lauren and Kevin for reading, cheering and supporting me and this novel. Your friendships are irreplaceable.

Lastly, I have to give a major shout out to Margaret Diehl who did a beautiful edit. Your hard work and helpful guidance was more than I could ask for.

Connect with me on your favorite social media outlet and let me know what you thought of the novel using #RoseofDancé
Facebook.com/authorerikasams
Facebook.com/roseofdance
Instagram @authorerikasams
Twitter @unicornandlatte

unicornhairandlattes.com

9 780692 194867